Pink Smoke and Mirrors

A Witch's Cove Mystery
Book 11

Vella Day

Pink smoke billowing out of my favorite bookstore sets me and my talking pink iguana on the trail of the arsonist. Watch out Witch's Cove.

Hi, I'm Glinda Goodall, amateur sleuth and witch. Whenever a fellow Witch's Cove resident is targeted, for whatever reason, I, along with my trusty familiar, Iggy, and my computer savvy boyfriend, Jaxson, always step up to the plate to solve the crime. Today will be no different.

This time it's Frank and Betty Sanchez's bookstore that was set ablaze, but for the life of me, I can't figure out why. Candle's Bookstore is one of the town's icons. I don't care that the gossip queens are convinced Frank, himself, set his place on fire. I refuse to believe I and plan to prove them wrong.

For once, it doesn't look like magic is involved, but I've been wrong before. Regardless of how the blaze was set, I might have to use magic to catch the criminal before the rest of the town goes up in flames.

Chapter One

IGGY'S SMALL ANIMAL claws scraped down my face, rousing me from slumber. "Glinda, wake up," he said.

It took a second to realize that my pink familiar was on my bed—in my space. I cracked open an eye, expecting sunlight to be pouring into the room. Instead, darkness surrounded me. I might have rolled over and ignored my iguana, except that Iggy never woke me in the middle of the night without cause.

When my brain finally engaged, I jerked awake. "What is it?"

"I smell smoke."

"In the apartment?" I don't know why I asked. Smoke was smoke. I inhaled but detected nothing.

"No. It's outside. Something's on fire down the street."

My pulse sped up. I could have asked him which building was ablaze, but I wanted to see for myself. I threw off the covers and raced to the window. Pink smoke was billowing from the rooftop of some building down the street, only I couldn't be certain which one it was. And why the pink color?

A blaring siren raced toward town from the north. Good. The fire department was coming. Heart racing, I flipped on the overhead light, pulled off my pajamas, and tossed on some clothes.

"Can I come with you?" Iggy asked.

"Your lungs can't take the smoke." Mine probably couldn't either, but I could protect myself better.

"Take pictures."

"It's pitch black. Sit on the ledge and watch. You won't miss a thing."

He waddled over to the window, and I lifted him onto the sill, even though he could climb up by himself.

I grabbed a sweater in case it was chilly, but if there was fire, I imagine I wouldn't need one. I could only hope this was a kitchen fire and not something more sinister, but at four in the morning, I wasn't holding my breath for a good outcome.

I ran down the staircase and out the side entrance to the alleyway that separated the Tiki Hut Grill where my apartment was located and the Cove Mortuary that my parents owned.

As soon as I made it to the main street, the sheriff's car pulled in front of…oh, no…Candles Bookstore. That was one of Witch's Cove's icons. I'd bought books there since I was a kid.

Along with Jaxson Harrison, I ran the Pink Iguana Sleuths agency, and I'd be using all my sleuthing and witch abilities to find out who did this—assuming it was arson and not caused by faulty wiring or something. That was a possibility since the building was rather ancient.

When I made it across the street, our deputy, Nash Solano, stopped me. "You can't get any closer, Glinda. It's not safe."

I couldn't see any flames or feel the heat. The entire interior appeared to be filled with pink smoke, though. "What's going on?"

"I'd like to ask you that."

"Me?" He couldn't think that because pink was my signature color that I was involved in this.

"Why are you out here in the middle of the night?" he asked.

"Iggy woke me up saying he smelled smoke. That motivated me to get out of bed, and when I spotted the pink color, I couldn't help but investigate." I clasped his arm. "You don't think I had anything to do with this, do you? You have to know that I love this bookstore."

"I can't say one way or another."

Couldn't or wouldn't? Just then Aaron Reed, one of the firefighters, motioned that he needed to speak with Nash, giving me a moment to observe what was going on—which wasn't much. The two of them chatted for a moment and then Nash returned. "Excuse me, Glinda, but duty calls. Please go home. There is nothing to see or do here."

Easy for him to say. I should have let Iggy come with me. He could have cloaked himself and then listened in on their conversation without being detected. But alas, Iggy was watching from my bedroom window. Not wanting to be hauled in for being a suspected arsonist, I headed back across the street.

By now, two or three other folks had come to gawk. Considering a small group was gathering, with probably more to come, tomorrow would be soon enough to find out what happened. Since no ambulance had arrived, and none of the adjacent stores seemed to have been harmed, there probably was nothing for me to do—at least not tonight.

No surprise, when I returned to the apartment, Iggy was pacing the living room.

"Well?" he asked.

"There's not much to tell other than the bookstore is filled with smoke. If I had to guess, I'd say the back room caught on fire."

"I thought smoke was gray."

"It is. Frank must have kept some chemicals back there that caused the pink color." Why a bookstore owner would have chemicals was anyone's guess. I yawned. "I'm sure by tomorrow, the town will be abuzz with what happened. I'm going to try to get some shuteye. I suggest you do the same."

I headed toward my bedroom, happy that Iggy seemed content to leave the questions until morning. Unfortunately, it wasn't long before a knock sounded on my apartment door. Because it wasn't a strong sound, I assumed it was my Aunt Fern who lived across the hall come to check on me—or rather to give me the latest update since she was one of the main gossip queens in town. My aunt owned the Tiki Hut Grill, along with the two apartments that resided above it, and she had probably learned what had happened last night.

I swung my legs over the bed, but before I had the chance to stand, my aunt came into my bedroom.

"Excuse the intrusion," she said. "Iggy crawled out of the cat door and gave me your key so I could let myself in."

I'd given her a spare key, but she must have forgotten. "No problem. I trust you heard about the fire at the bookstore?" I asked.

I scooted over on the bed and patted the space next to me.

She sat down. "Of course, I did. Pearl called me. How did you hear about it?"

Being close to eighty, Pearl Dillsmith was the oldest of the local gossip queens. She also was the sheriff's dispatcher as well as his grandmother.

"After Iggy smelled the smoke around four in the morning, I checked it out, but I couldn't see much. Did you get the deets on what happened?"

"From what I heard, no one was injured, but between the fire hoses and the sprinklers, all of the books were ruined."

My heart ached for Frank and Betty Sanchez. They'd run that store for as long as I could remember. "How terrible. Did Steve have any idea what happened?"

Pearl probably knew everything her grandson did, and if she knew, the town's gossips knew. "It was arson," my aunt said.

I sucked in a breath. "Arson? I was actually hoping the microwave in back had short-circuited or something."

Aunt Fern lifted her chin. "Want to know what I think?"

"Always."

"I think Frank set the fire himself."

I barked out a laugh. "Seriously? Why? That bookstore is his life."

"There are many reasons. The first is that he is in his seventies, and he wants to retire."

That was lame. "He could sell his inventory and the goodwill that goes with it. Burning it down is rather extreme."

My aunt shook her head. "He's been renting the space all these years and is behind in his rent payments, or so I've heard. Don't you remember when Betty told you that she and

Frank had asked their son for money to help them out?"

"Yes, but he turned them down, or so she claimed. No one was able to corroborate that request, though." Her son, Daniel Sanchez, had been a wealthy lawyer in Miami who was murdered shortly after that conversation.

She shrugged. "I imagine they still owe money to Heath Richards, the building's new owner."

"How does ruining your business help you pay your bills?" I didn't want to think Frank was guilty of anything.

"Insurance money for the lost inventory."

"They won't pay if Frank set the fire."

Aunt Fern painted on her Mona Lisa smile. "You don't know?"

Clearly, I must not. "Know what?"

"Frank Sanchez was the fire chief some twenty or thirty years ago. He would know how to cover his tracks."

"What? Bookstore owner Frank Sanchez was the fire chief? How did I not know this?"

My aunt clasped my hand. "You were merely a child back then."

"Why did he quit?" I don't know why it mattered now, though.

"I don't recall."

Uh-huh. Sure, she didn't. My aunt remembered everything—except that I'd given her my spare key. Not to worry, there were others who would spill the beans. "Thanks for the update."

My aunt stood. "I'd hate for it to be Frank. I really would. That means you and Jaxson need to find out who did this."

"I'll give it my best." And I would too.

Once she left, I redressed and then headed over to the office. If Jaxson hadn't picked up any chatter about the fire, we'd stop over at the diner, the tea shop, or the coffee shop to see what the other gossip queens had to say. The fire—or smoke bomb—happened five hours ago. Surely, that was enough time for people to spread the word about who might have been responsible.

When Iggy and I arrived at the office, my eighteen-year old cousin, Rihanna, had already left for school, leaving Jaxson alone at his desk. He turned around. "I trust you heard about the fire?"

"I sure did." I explained how Iggy had woken me up in the middle of the night and how I'd rushed over to investigate.

"Learn anything?"

Considering the website he had up showed pink smoke, he'd learned about that aspect of the crime. "Not much other than Aaron Reed appeared to be first on the scene."

"Aaron, huh? What did he have to say?"

Aaron graduated a year ahead of Jaxson. I didn't know many of Jaxson's classmates since he was six years older than me, but he'd mentioned Aaron a few times. The man had been trouble, almost as much as Jaxson himself.

"He was busy chatting with Nash. I don't think he saw me."

"The two of us might have to have a talk—for old times' sake, of course."

"I didn't think you liked each other," I said.

Jaxson huffed. "Kids like us didn't like anyone. I think we respected each other, though, since we both disregarded the rules back then."

"What made him change?" Jaxson wasn't the same person after he'd been accused of robbing a liquor store and then had to spend three years in jail before finally being exonerated. Thankfully, our former sheriff finally admitted he'd trumped up the charges to avoid accusing his son.

"Who's to say he is any different now?"

"He's a fireman. Police and firemen are civil servants. They are supposed to be noble."

His chuckle sounded rueful. "If I recall, the past sheriff and deputy of Witch's Cove were civil servants, and they were as corrupt as they came."

"That's true." One was dead and the other was in jail. Time to get back to business. I nodded to the screen. "Whatcha got there."

"I was curious about the pink smoke."

"Me, too. Nash kind of joked about it having to do with me."

Jaxson shook his head. "I'm sure he was kidding."

"I hope so, unless someone is trying to frame me. I don't think I've made that many enemies, except for maybe all the people I've helped put behind bars."

He chuckled. "Let's explore that idea last." He tapped the screen. "It says here that pink smoke can be caused by the chemical, lithium chloride. It's used in smoke bombs to create the pink color."

"And if a smoke bomb was involved, can one of those even do much harm?"

"I don't know. It also says here that this chemical is used in auto repair for welding. The article then gives a bunch of chemical nonsense that I don't understand. Chemistry wasn't my best subject."

"I loved science, but maybe Christian Durango can help us."

"Because he is an auto mechanic?"

I shrugged. "Can't hurt to ask. He helped with our last case." His sister, who was fast becoming one of Rihanna's best friends, said his attitude toward life had improved quite a lot after being thought of in a positive light for a change.

"Let's talk to him. If nothing else, Christian might be able to ask around to see who has some of this chemical."

We headed over to the garage where Christian worked. He and I had graduated in the same class, yet until one of our fellow classmates had been murdered last month, I hadn't spoken to Christian in years.

It took less than ten minutes to reach his garage. "Let's hope he is working today."

"If not, I bet the boss can help us."

"True."

We parked and went inside where we found Christian changing the oil in a car.

"Hey, Christian." I tried to sound upbeat.

He spun around. For a moment, he looked as if he'd seen a ghost. "What are you guys doing here?" He seemed cautious yet friendly.

"Did you hear about the fire at Candles Bookstore?"

"No. I don't get into town much. What happened?"

I explained about the smoke I saw.

"What does that have to do with me?" This time his defenses had shot up.

Poor guy must have been wrongfully accused quite often in the past to have that kind of reaction.

Jaxson stepped forward. "I did some research. The smoke might have been caused by some lithium chloride igniting."

Christian whistled. "I've never used that stuff, but another one of our auto repair guys has. We use it as a brazing flux for aluminum, but it can be used for a lot of other repair work, too. I even heard it can be used as a drying agent for dehumidifiers. You'd have to ask a chemistry guy for the specifics."

The more ways to use it, the harder it would be to pin down who might have any. "Do you think we can speak with this other mechanic?"

"Glen's not in yet, but when he gets here, I can ask him about it and get back to you."

"Sounds great." This could be the lead we needed.

"Is that all?"

I nodded. "For now."

"Let me know if I can help in any way," Christian said.

How cool was it that he seemed to want to work with us again? "We will."

Since we learned the information we'd come for, Jaxson and I left. "He isn't telling us everything," Jaxson said as we headed to his truck.

"Why would you say that? I know Rihanna can read minds. Can you do that now?"

"Hardly, but he had a difficult time making eye contact."

"Maybe he's used to having people think the worst of him. Are you suggesting Christian had something to do with the burning of the bookstore?"

"Maybe, maybe not, but he is a warlock, don't forget."

"I bet he hasn't been in that store in ten years."

"Who's to say someone didn't hire him to use magic to set off a pink bomb and then light the fire?"

Jaxson's imagination was out of control. To be fair, Christian had used his warlock skills recently for no good. "I'd love to find out if a person with magical abilities could even do that, because if he can, I want to learn that trick."

Jaxson smiled. "That's my girl."

I wasn't sure what he meant by that, but I hoped he was just teasing me.

Chapter Two

"WANT TO GRAB some breakfast at the diner?" Jaxson asked as he backed out of the parking space.

He wasn't fooling me. Dolly Andrews, the owner of the Spellbound Diner, was an even bigger gossip than my aunt. "Of course, but you don't need an excuse to talk with Dolly."

He grinned. "You know me too well."

"I do." I loved that the two of us had developed such an easy going working relationship that we could say anything to each other.

We drove straight there. I would have asked Jaxson to stop at the office so we could have picked up Iggy, but I was quite certain my familiar could find something to eat on his own. The office had a cat door that allowed him to come and go. Because Iggy enjoyed hearing the gossip first hand, he usually wanted me to discuss it right then and there, which made me look a bit crazy to any outsiders. Only people with magic could hear him talk.

When we entered Dolly's diner, it was packed, but we got lucky and snagged a booth. "When we get back, I want to drag out the whiteboard and come up with a list of possible suspects."

Jaxson laughed. "How do you propose doing that since we

have no idea who burned down the bookstore?"

"That lack of knowledge has not stopped us before. We know that Frank had motive. That's one suspect."

"I'm thinking since he was a fire chief years ago, he'd have done something a little less flashy than a pink smoke bomb."

"You might be right."

As soon as Dolly was free, she rushed up to us. "I'm so glad you two stopped in."

"We're glad, too. Please tell me you know something about the incident at the bookstore last night—or rather early this morning," I said.

"I wish."

That was a change. "Didn't Pearl talk to you?"

"Of course she did, but I didn't believe a word of what she said."

What was going on? "Why is that? She's your go-to girl."

"Not this time. She's saying some pretty nasty things about Frank Sanchez, and I refuse to believe it." The owner crossed her arms over her chest and lifted her chin.

I'd never seen Dolly act like this before. Did she feel left out of the loop or something? If that was the reason, maybe I could help. "Does she think Frank set the fire because he used to be the fire chief?"

Dolly waved a hand. "Who knows what goes through that woman's head."

Now she had me intrigued. "What's caused Pearl to be so against Frank all of a sudden?"

"She doesn't talk about it much, but Frank and Pearl used to date."

Eww. I couldn't picture it, but maybe I didn't have a

good enough imagination. "Really?"

"Yes, but after almost a year of going out, he dumped her."

"Maybe it was because Pearl was quite a bit older than he was?"

Dolly's lips pressed together. "That didn't matter. Back in the day, Pearl was a real looker. What was a five-year age difference to a guy if the woman looked like Pearl and was smart to boot?"

"Are you implying she still holds a grudge after all these years? Come on, she married Mr. Dillsmith. She couldn't have pined for very long."

I'd only met the man a few times, but I don't remember if he was good-looking or not. As a teen, I wasn't interested in old men.

"I wouldn't say it's a grudge, exactly, but more like she doesn't give Frank the benefit of the doubt when it comes to some things."

"That's a shame." When Frank's son had recently been murdered, Pearl hadn't shown any signs of being angry at him. Why the change of heart? "What's your take on the fire? Do you have any suspects?"

Dolly's eyes sparkled. "Well, now that you ask, I might be able to come up with one or two names, but just so you know, I have no proof."

"Join the club," I said. "Who's your number one suspect?"

"The arson investigator."

Had I had been drinking my tea, I might have spit it out. "The arson inspector? Why on Earth would you pick Ian Silver?"

Her eyes grew wide. "You don't know, do you? Of course you don't. You weren't even born."

Seems like a lot happened back then. "What? Tell us."

She looked over her shoulder, probably to see if she needed to take care of any customers, but everyone seemed to be doing okay. "Kevin Silver, Ian Silver's dad, was a great fireman. That's not to say Frank wasn't good, but everyone agreed that Kevin should have been the one promoted when their chief retired."

"Don't tell me the mayor picked Frank instead?"

"You betcha. It was mostly because Mayor Sinclair was Jane Collin's father."

I held up my hands in the form of a T. "Time out. Jane Collins as in Collins Insurance?"

"The one and only. I need to back up here."

"Please do. I'm totally confused."

"Remember I said that Frank dumped Pearl?"

We were back to her? "Yes."

"He dumped her for Jane."

"Is Frank's love life from his youth really that relevant now?" Jaxson asked.

"I'm afraid so. You see, most of the women loved Frank. I personally was too young to be smitten, but back then, he was the bees knees."

I must not have gotten enough sleep, because her second explanation didn't make any more sense than the first. "So, Frank dumps Pearl for Jane. Then what?"

"A year later, Jane finds the love of her life—the man she ended up marrying—and dumps Frank."

Maybe he had it coming, but I didn't say anything. "Was

he upset?"

She shrugged. "All I know is that Jane felt bad for ditching him and asked her father, the mayor, to appoint Frank as fire chief—instead of Kevin Silver."

I looked over at Jaxson and smiled. "Ah, I get it now. You good?"

"I think so." He turned to Dolly. "Why would you think Ian is upset at Frank now? All this happened, what, twenty-five or thirty years ago?" He held up a hand. "I guess I should ask when did Frank quit the fire department? For as long as I can remember, Frank and Betty have always run the bookstore."

"About twenty years ago, but all those emotions might have been stirred up when Ian's dad passed away a few months back."

I whistled. I remembered Mr. Silver's death. He'd died of a heart attack. No foul play was suspected. "Do you have any proof that the arson investigator is involved?"

"No, and that's the problem. It's just my best guess, but I will keep my ears open."

She looked so sad. "I get it. I'm in the guessing stage right now too."

I waited for her to tell me her second choice for arsonist, but, instead, she pulled out her pad and took our order.

"What do you think?" I asked Jaxson as soon as Dolly left.

"It's a stretch at best. Does Ian Silver have a reason to dislike Frank? Sure, but that was a beef between Ian's dad and Frank, not between him and Frank."

"I know, but if my dad had unresolved issues with someone and then died, I might want to pick up the crusade." That was another stretch, considering Frank had long since left the fire department.

Jaxson dipped his chin. "By setting fire to someone's livelihood?"

"I guess that is a bit harsh."

"You think? Slash the guy's tires, key his car, or break the storefront window. Do something that is fixable. Don't burn down the whole store. If I recall, Frank and Betty had a lot of one-of-a-kind used books in there."

I didn't dare ask about the last time he'd been in the bookstore. Jaxson relied on his computer for research. "They did. When we finish eating, how about we check out the damage? I couldn't tell much when I was there last night."

"Sounds good. Has Andorra called?"

"Why would she call?" Andorra was Drake's girlfriend. "Did your brother say something?"

"No, but the Hex and Bones Apothecary is next to the Candles Bookstore. I was wondering if maybe some smoke got into their store?"

I sucked in a breath. "I hadn't even thought of that." I was losing it. If we hadn't just ordered, I might have suggested we leave right away. Instead, I did the next best thing—I pulled out my phone and called her.

"Hey, Glinda."

I couldn't tell her frame of mind from the greeting alone. "Is your store okay after last night's fire?"

"You heard about that, did you? Erase that. Of course, you did. Yes, we are fine. I tried to find out some information, but even my grandmother is hitting a stonewall."

"Wow. The well of knowledge has died up all because

Pearl is convinced that Frank set his place on fire?" I remembered to keep my voice down this time.

"What? No. My grandmother is sensing something else, but she can't put her finger on it."

If Bertha Murdoch was getting a strange feeling, maybe magic was involved. "Has she, or you, ever heard of witches using fire before? I mean, we are capable of striking a match, but can you wish something to go up in flames?"

"I don't know anyone with that ability, but that's not to say someone couldn't do it."

"I see."

"While I have you on the line, you'll never guess who showed up when I came into work today?" Andorra said.

More guessing games—something I disliked—but I wanted to give it a try. "Hugo?"

"Yes."

Uh-oh. Hugo was Andorra's familiar who spent most of his life as a stone gargoyle. He only appeared in his human form when Andorra was in danger. "That's not good. Did he say why he'd transformed?"

"He changed when he smelled the smoke."

"Could he sense who might have been at the bookstore in the middle of the night?" Since Hugo never left the store, he might have heard or seen something.

"No, but the person used the back entrance. Hugo could tell that much since our storage room is right next to the bookstore's rear entrance."

I'd have to ask the sheriff if the bookstore's back door was broken into. "That's good intel. Maybe later, we can chat with Hugo."

She chuckled. "Bring Iggy. I know Hugo enjoys having him around."

"Will do." I disconnected and told Jaxson what she said.

"It's a relief that their store wasn't targeted too."

"I know. I was thinking that if the bookstore's back door was jimmied, it might mean Frank wasn't involved."

"I'm not so—"

One of the servers delivered our drinks. "Your meals will be right up."

"Thanks." I turned back to Jaxson. "You were saying."

"Frank might have pretended to break into his shop to make us think it wasn't him."

I sipped my tea. "True. We definitely need to see how much damage was done."

"Would a lot of damage imply Frank was innocent or guilty?"

Jaxson always tested my theories. "I don't know, but I would think the less damage, the higher the probability that Frank is guilty. He could get the insurance money, pay off what he owes, and then buy more used books to replace the ones he lost."

Jaxson flashed me a quick smile. "Good thinking."

I could tell he wasn't buying it, though, but time would tell. Our breakfast arrived, and I scarfed it down. I waited for Dolly to return with some revelation, but she'd disappeared into the back and remained there. I had to hope the other gossip queens would tell us more.

After we finished, we parked back at the office and gathered Iggy. "Hugo has requested your presence."

"He's back?" I hadn't heard Iggy this excited since he first met his girlfriend, Aimee, the talking cat, about nine months ago.

"Apparently, but Hugo transformed because he sensed danger—or rather smoke. I thought maybe you two could chat about what he knows."

My familiar puffed out his chest. "Leave Hugo to me."

I laughed. "You are a piece of work, Iggy Goodall."

"I don't know why you'd say that. Besides Andorra, I'm the only one who can communicate with him."

I sobered. "You're right. Ready to see what the bookstore looks like and what Hugo has to say?"

He lifted his leg and tapped his head, which was as close to a salute as he could get. "You betcha."

Chapter Three

"**I**T'S WORSE THAN I thought," I announced.

Jaxson, Iggy, and I stood in front of the Candles Bookstore assessing the damage. One of the two front windows had been broken, though someone had been kind enough to board it up. I wasn't sure if the heat from the fire had shattered the glass, or if the firemen needed to break it for easy access. When I'd arrived last night, all I saw was smoke— no flames.

No wonder Nash told me to leave. The area had been dangerous.

Jaxson pressed his face to the unharmed window. "Uh-oh. The water damage is extensive."

"Really?" I moved next to him, and when I looked in, my heart broke. Jaxson was right. The place was a disaster. Frank and Betty worked so hard to make this a great store, and now everything was lost. I tried seeing into the back room, but someone had placed plastic across the entrance. No telling what had happened back there. I pressed my ear to the glass and listened. "Are those voices I hear?"

"I believe so. I can see some lights flashing, too. The investigators must be doing their job. Let's hope they can figure out how the fire started. That could help lead us to the arsonist."

"Knowing how the fire started won't point a finger at the guilty party—assuming Aunt Fern has her facts right about this fire having been deliberately set."

"We'll see," Jaxson said.

"Can I visit Hugo now?" Iggy asked as he poked his head out of my purse, clearly not caring if he interrupted our conversation or not.

"Sure."

He planted a claw over his nose. "Phew. It stinks."

I could barely smell the fire. Then again, I wasn't an animal. I turned to Jaxson. "I hope it's true that there are firewalls between each of the stores. They'd prevent the fire from spreading."

"I'm impressed if that's true. These buildings are old."

"Maybe it happened during the last remodel."

He nodded. "Maybe. What I want to know is who called it in, because the fire department sure responded fast, especially since you saw no flames when you arrived," Jaxson said.

"I thought the same thing. How did the caller know there was even a fire?"

"Someone had to have seen the pink smoke."

"At four in the morning?" I asked.

Jaxson shrugged. "It's almost as if the arsonist wanted someone to call it in."

That made no sense. "Why? I thought the purpose of arson was to destroy the building."

"I wasn't thinking. You're right."

I turned around to see who might have been up at four—

other than my iguana—to make that call. "The Psychics Corner is directly across the street, but they would have been closed at that hour. Had it not been for Iggy and his excellent nose, I wouldn't have known about it."

"Jennifer Larson works the late shift at the sheriff's department, but she's home by two in the morning," he said. "Who answers the 911 calls in the middle of the night, do you think?"

"Nash mentioned that the calls go directly to either him or Steve. You don't happen to have any buddies in the fire department you could ask, do you?" I had the sense the sheriff's department might not share that information with us.

"Other than Aaron—who I can't even claim is a friend— no. It's been years since we've spoken."

That was because Jaxson only returned to Witch's Cove a year ago. "It can't hurt to give him a call. He was definitely one of the first on the scene if not the first one to get there. He might know who called it in."

"I'll see if he's willing to talk." Jaxson placed a hand on my back and escorted me next door to the Hex and Bones shop.

When I walked in, a hint of smoke lingered in the air, despite the sweet smell of the incense. Thankfully, there didn't appear to be any damage.

Iggy poked his head up. "It stinks in here, too."

"Really?"

"Uh-huh. Kind of bad."

I wondered if Iggy was just saying that to get attention, or if it was true and I just couldn't smell it? I placed him on the floor, and he waddled off toward the back room to find Hugo.

No customers were standing near the cash register to see him, which I considered a good thing. Some people might freak out if they spotted my pink cutie running free.

I was happy for Iggy. I had no doubt that he and Hugo would have a good conversation.

Drake's girlfriend finished up with a customer and came over. When I spotted her grandmother coming out of the back room, I waved. As always, I was happy to see Bertha Murdock, the owner, back in town.

Andorra and I hugged. "Did you learn anything about the fire?" she asked.

"Not a lot, but I was hoping Hugo might have sensed something," I said.

"No, just what I told you over the phone."

"I thought he only transformed from stone to flesh when he believed you were in danger."

"I asked him about that, but he said he didn't think I was in immediate danger as much as he was worried about the store catching fire."

"I can understand that. Regardless of why he became human again, I know Iggy will be happy to see his friend. It's possible he can help Hugo do a little self-discovery about the event. Sometimes asking the right questions can trigger a memory."

She chuckled. "Let's hope so. What I do know is that Hugo misses Iggy. Your familiar is his one and only friend."

Aww. "Any time Hugo decides to give up his stone facade, I can bring Iggy here."

She smiled. "Hugo might even change for that visit."

"Did Bertha figure out what might have happened or,

rather, who might be responsible for the fire?"

"Other than she *sensed something*? She didn't say, but let's see if her witch radar has kicked into gear yet. I'll ask Elizabeth if she is willing to man the store while we chat."

"How nice to have three of you working here now," Jaxson said.

"Totally." Andorra took off to speak with her cousin.

I had no idea why I checked out who was browsing the store. It wasn't as if I thought the arsonist would be doing a bit of occult shopping while scoping out his next site. Habit, I guess.

I snapped my fingers. "I have a crazy idea."

Jaxson chuckled. "It's one of the things I love about you—all of your out-of-the-box theories. Tell me your latest."

"Do we know if Mr. Richards owns the entire strip of stores or just Frank's bookstore?"

"It isn't something I ever inquired about. Why?"

"What if Mr. Richards was trying to get rid of his current tenant, and the only way to do that was to scare the Sanchezes into leaving?"

Jaxson stared at me for a moment. "By burning them out?" He waved a dismissive hand. "Why not just raise their rent?"

"Years ago, I recall hearing he can't change the rate, but I could be wrong. I thought it was written into the lease that as long as a tenant wants to stay, the rent must remain the same. It's like those rent-controlled apartments in New York City."

"Interesting idea. Bertha must know."

"For sure."

Andorra returned. "Come on back. Memaw is anxious to

chat about this terrible event."

Bertha had set up a few chairs and invited us to sit down. "How are you doing, dear? It's been a while," she said.

She seemed calm—almost too calm—but that might be her way of covering up her anxiety. "Good. I'm keeping busy."

We chatted a bit more, but I sensed Bertha wanted to get to what was really bothering her. "Before we start trying to figure out who might have set the fire next door, can I ask if you rent or own this space?"

"That's an odd question, but I don't mind telling you. I rent. Because I've been here for a long, long time, I hardly pay anything. I will never move—or rather I could never afford to move."

"The rent is that cheap?"

"Oh, my yes. The owner's father, Ben, gave us a great deal, because he was desperate to fill the space when he first developed these stores."

"Does he own the whole strip of stores then?"

"He does, or rather, he did. He recently passed, and his son, Heath, now runs the company."

"Good to know."

"Ben Richards also promised the rent would never change," Bertha announced.

My memory had been right. "That might have been foolish on his part."

"In hindsight, I think it was," Bertha said. "I've been here twenty years. That's a lot of savings on my part."

"Is his son planning to increase the rent somehow?" Jaxson asked.

"He's trying to, but I think he knows when he's defeated. A contract is a contract. I haven't read it in many years, but it mentions something about if Ben Richard died, his son would honor the rent rate."

I kind of felt sorry for the guy. "What if there are repairs, like the need for a new roof or new plumbing? Repairing something that big could put him into debt."

"Ben always managed, but maybe it was because the tenants took care of the small things. When he was alive, we didn't need a lot of major work, but the day will come when something big needs to be replaced."

"What happens to the rent if you move?" Jaxson asked.

"It nullifies the contract. Mr. Richards can change it to whatever he wants—or rather to whatever the market will bear."

I looked over at Jaxson. "I'm curious if Mr. Richards tried to get Betty and Frank to move."

"What are you suggesting? That Frank turned him down, and Heath Richards wanted to convince him in another way?" she asked.

"Maybe. Is that so crazy?"

Bertha blew out a breath. "I'd have to think about that. Frank did tell me he recently spoke with Heath about some money problems, but he didn't give me any specifics. However, since his rent is cheap, I don't think his problems would stem from that."

All good information, but I needed more. I hoped that since she was about Frank's age, she might be able to add a bit of background information on him. "What can you tell me about Frank and his early days?" Dolly sure seemed to think his past was pertinent.

Her eyes widened. "Why do you want to know about that?"

I told her about Aunt Fern and Pearl's theories that Frank might have set the fire himself in order to get the insurance money for the contents of his store. "Being a former fire chief, he had the knowledge and ability to pull it off."

"Nonsense."

"What part of it is nonsense?" Jaxson asked.

"Most of it. Frank would never do that. He knows a fire would devastate Betty. She loves the store. Secondly, the part about Frank not deserving to be fire chief is also wrong."

Her passion impressed me. "Why is that?"

"Right out of high school, Frank enlisted in the Army so he could fight in Vietnam. He won a Medal of Honor for his bravery, too. He was more than deserving to be chief."

I whistled. "I had no idea."

"Few do. Those were difficult times. I doubt even his grandson has heard the tales," she said. "I think it's hard for Frank to talk about it."

His grandson was dating Rihanna. Now that Gavin was living in Witch's Cove, at least for the year, he and Frank would hopefully grow closer. It would be nice if he shared with Gavin what happened in the war.

"What about Ian Silver's dad?" Jaxson asked. "You don't think he would have made a good chief?"

"He most definitely would have. He was a Marine who was a weapons expert."

"That training would translate well into being a fireman," I said.

"Absolutely. To be honest, it was a toss-up between the two men. Those who favored Kevin believed that Frank only received the promotion because he was shown some favoritism by the mayor."

That matched what Dolly said. "Was Mr. Silver angry when he didn't get the job?"

"Kevin? No. He was too honorable. He understood that someone had to win and someone had to lose. He also knew that Jane had been sweet on Frank. It made sense that her dad would appoint Frank, despite those two having broken up." Bertha lifted her head, giving me the impression she liked Kevin. A lot.

"My aunt said she thought Frank was planning to retire. Did he ever mention that to you?

"No, though he told me that Betty's knees were giving her trouble, and that managing the bookstore was becoming more and more difficult for her. He hinted that he was having some health problems, too, but I don't have any details."

"If that were the case, there would be no need for Heath to hurry Frank along in selling his inventory, assuming Frank was planning to do it anyway," I said.

"Maybe," she said.

Jaxson tilted his head. "Could Frank afford to retire, though? Sure, they might have social security and some retirement benefits from him serving, but if they had medical expenses, it could be rough."

"I don't know about any of that," Bertha said.

I turned to Jaxson. "It's possible Aunt Fern doesn't know what she's talking about. Frank might not be as destitute as she implied—or he could be. We just don't know." Sometimes I wonder if my aunt was getting a bit out of touch. "Bertha, Andorra said you had a *sense* about this fire. What was that about?"

"I wish I knew. I'll admit that I'm scared that the store next to mine was targeted, but was it because of something Frank and Betty did, or because someone wants to drive Frank out of his space for another reason? All I know is that I'm petrified I will be next."

"That would scare anyone. I'm sure the sheriff will use all of his resources to solve this crime."

"What if magic is involved?" Jaxson shot out.

I looked over at him. He shrugged, implying it was not an unreasonable suggestion. "I don't think a witch is needed to light a match, but that is not to say we can't catch this person using some spell," I said.

"You're right," Bertha said. "I personally have never met a witch or warlock who can say a spell and cause a flame to appear. Then again, I'd never met anyone who could disappear or move a lock with his mind before, either."

"Excellent point. I'll check with Levy. He and his coven have a library of old spells that are amazing." He knew people who could cloak themselves and open doors using mental telepathy, which was what Bertha was referring to.

She sighed. "I'd love to see that library someday."

I smiled. "Maybe that can be arranged."

"That would be great, but we have to consider that the arsonist could be an ordinary human," she said.

"I know."

"Tell me, how are you going to go about finding this arsonist—whether he be a witch, a warlock, or a regular fella?"

Bertha asked.

"I wish I knew. Dolly is thinking the arson investigator is responsible whereas my aunt and Pearl are convinced it's Frank. It seems as if he is at the center of our arson plot, whether he was involved directly or not."

Bertha's lips pinched. "Let's keep an open mind."

She sounded like Jaxson and Drake. "Maybe we should speak with Jane Collins since I believe Frank has his inventory insured with her company."

"I think we all do. Back in the days, she was the only one around."

"Are they still in touch?" I asked.

"I've seen Frank and Jane chatting a time or two. Most likely it was about business, but maybe he was discussing other issues with her."

"Her husband died three years ago, if I remember correctly," I said.

"Yes. It left a big hole in her heart. Frank and Betty visited her often to help her get through the crisis."

"How wonderful. Good friends like that are hard to find." No way would a man as compassionate as Frank torch his own place.

We chatted a bit more, but we'd exhausted Bertha's knowledge of who might want to set fire to Candles Bookstore.

After thanking her and collecting Iggy, we left.

As soon as we stepped outside, I asked Iggy if he had learned anything.

"Hugo got a rather strange vibe the night of the fire, which was why he changed into his human form."

That wasn't a lot to go on. "Did he think that either Andorra, Elizabeth, or Bertha were in danger?" Andorra said it was because he'd smelled smoke that he'd turned human—or rather human-like.

"Hugo wasn't sure, but they could have been."

I looked over at Jaxson. "I meant to check for any surveillance cameras in the Hex and Bones store. Did you notice if there were any?"

"No, but that's not to say there aren't. I was focused on other things."

"Me, too. If Bertha doesn't have any, we should suggest she install some. Even if the fire was a one-time event, if someone steals something in her store, it could help identify the thief."

"I'm sure after the fire, she'll be open to the suggestion."

"Do you want to see what Jane Collins has to say about the fire and Frank?"

"I have no problem with that, but do you think she can talk about a client's case?"

I smiled. "Only one way to find out."

Jaxson wrapped an arm around my waist. "A sleuth to the core."

Chapter Four

AFTER DROPPING IGGY off at my apartment so he could give Aimee the details about Hugo and the fire, we drove to Collins' Insurance, which was about a mile out of town in another strip mall. From the lack of upkeep to the exterior, her company wasn't doing all that well, which was a real shame. I wanted to see every business succeed.

Once we stepped inside, I wasn't sure what the most effective way to approach Jane about Frank would be. Should I even bring up the possibility that Frank might have set his place on fire? Maybe not. Perhaps I just needed to get her to talk about him in general.

The reception area was empty, but directly behind the desk was an office with its door open. Inside was a woman who looked to be about Frank's age. She probably was Jane Collins.

The gray-haired woman looked up, smiled, and pushed back her chair. As she came around her desk to greet us, she appeared quite spry.

"How can I help you?"

We introduced ourselves. "Jaxson and I run the Pink Iguana Sleuth agency, and we are trying to find out what happened to Frank Sanchez's bookstore."

Her face seemed to freeze, but only for a moment. "Yes, of course. It was such a tragedy. Please come in, though I'm not sure what I can tell you. Client confidentiality and all."

"I understand." We followed her into her office and took the seats in front of her desk. Her desk nameplate stated this was the owner. "I don't know why you'd know, but since you and Frank were friends at one time, can you guess who might have wanted to set his store on fire?"

She blew out a breath. "I couldn't even hazard a guess. Has it been confirmed yet that it was arson? It hasn't even been half a day."

"Not officially, but it's rumored to be." It was disappointing Jane didn't point a finger at anyone, but she might not be willing to name someone right off the bat. She was a professional, after all. "I trust Frank had insurance for the contents of his store?" Besides books, Betty and Frank carried items like calendars, candles, notebooks, and seasonal specialties.

"He did."

I was kind of hoping she'd tell me how much the policy was worth, but she remained closed-mouth. "Do you know who insured the building, which is owned by Heath Richards?"

"Not my firm. I imagine he's still using Anderson Insurance over in Summertime. Heath's daddy and Josh Anderson were good friends."

Ben Richards seemed like a loyal man. "I'm sorry I didn't know Heath's father."

"He was a big contributor to the growth of our downtown—at least he was when he lived in Witch's Cove." Her lips pressed together.

"And his son?"

She shook her head. "I only met him a few times, but he is only out for a buck."

"What do you mean?" Jaxson asked.

He knew, but he must have wanted to keep her talking. "You didn't hear it from me, but Heath is trying to raise everyone's rent—a lot."

"I thought his dad had a contract with everyone that stated he couldn't alter the rent as long as they were current tenants," I said.

"He did, which is why what Heath is doing is not very nice—though it is legal."

"What is he doing? Not repairing the place?"

"More or less. The renters fix all of the small things, but he's been real slow when it comes to repairing major issues, like the out-of-date wiring and the leaky roof. I mean, he fixes the stuff, but too often the job is done on the cheap."

That matched what Bertha said, which made me wonder if the fire wasn't arson at all. "What happens if a tenant doesn't fix a leak or take care of small damages, for example?" Jaxson asked.

"They can face eviction."

Interesting. "Is the damage from the fire Frank's responsibility or the building owner's?"

"That depends on the cause. My insurance company, along with Mr. Richard's insurance company will have to discuss it, but Frank won't have to pay a dime beyond his deductible."

This implied there would be no reason for Frank to set his

own place on fire. The only benefit would be the ability to purchase recently released books, which might not be a bad thing. He and Betty didn't always order the newest titles in a timely fashion. However, if Betty was having a hard time getting around, Frank might have agreed to sell the bookstore, assuming anyone wanted to buy it.

Since we weren't getting anywhere with this line of questioning, I thought I'd bring up Ian Silver's alleged beef with Frank. "Someone suggested that maybe Ian Silver, the arson investigator, wanted to drive Frank out of town, because of what happened between him and Ian's dad, Kevin." Okay, I made up the part about wanting Frank to leave Witch's Cove, but I was interested to see how she responded.

"Why would he do that? Everyone loves Frank."

Was she one of those people? If so, she wouldn't be the arsonist—not that she'd ever been a suspect. Burning down a store she insured wouldn't be smart either, unless she wanted to help Frank out once more.

"Ian's dad died recently. He might want to avenge his father for not having been selected fire chief all those years ago."

Jane's face turned red as she lifted her chin. "Nonsense. That's ancient history."

"What can you tell us about Frank and Pearl? That break-up seemed contentious," Jaxson said.

I hoped he wasn't thinking Pearl had anything to do with the fire. She had too much to lose. If her grandson caught her, Steve was too honorable to look the other way.

"Not much. Romances come and romances go."

"Pearl seems quite certain that Frank was the arsonist," I

said. "Why would she suggest that if she wasn't angry with him?"

Jane huffed out a breath. "Maybe because when her husband passed away, Frank didn't offer her much sympathy."

"Like he did with you." I made it a statement rather than a question.

"Yes, Betty and Frank took real good care of me after John died."

I couldn't remember when Pearl's husband died exactly, but that might have something to do with her issue with Frank. Or did it?

I raised my brows at Jaxson to see if he had any other questions, but he subtly shook his head. "Thank you for your time. If you hear of anything that might help us help Frank, here's our business card." I pulled one out of my purse and handed it to her.

"I will let you know if I learn anything."

Once back in the car, I sank against the seat. "That was a bust."

"Not necessarily. The packets may not have made that big of an impact on the fire and needed a larger quantity to make that much pink smoke. The packets may have been a diversion."

"I guess." I wasn't seeing it though.

"Not only that, but I now understand the business model a bit better as to why Ben Richards charged such little rent."

"Why? Because he wouldn't have to deal with the day-to-day repairs?"

"In large part," Jaxson said.

"I wonder how many stores are still run by the original

owners? If the only two old timers are Frank and Bertha, she needs to be careful."

"I totally agree. I'll do a little investigating." Jaxson started the car. "Where to?"

I was about to say that we should stop at the tea shop for a drink and some gossip when my phone rang. I lifted it out of my pocket, surprised that it was Christian Durango, our garage mechanic. "Christian?"

"Glinda, Glen is here at the garage, and he needs to show you something."

That was intriguing. I was about to ask Jaxson if he minded going there, but he must have heard the request, because without me asking, he pulled out of the parking lot and drove toward Christian's work place. "We'll be right there." I disconnected.

"I wonder why Christian couldn't just tell you over the phone about the lithium chloride, if that's what this is about," Jaxson said.

I shrugged. "Christian might love a good mystery."

Since we were close to his shop already, we arrived a few minutes later and found our caller inside. I expected Christian to be excited at having found a clue, but he appeared rather somber.

"Why the secrecy?" I asked him.

He motioned Glen to come over. "This is Glen Harmony. Glen, why don't you tell them what you found."

He nodded. "When I arrived this morning, Christian asked me about the chemical that was possibly used in the blaze. I went over to the storage unit and found someone had broken in and stolen what we had. I'll show you."

That must be why we needed to be there. We walked to the other side of the bay where the door to the locker had been dented. "Either the thief is inexperienced, or he is trying to make us think he is," I said. The lock looked easy to pick for someone with experience.

"My thoughts exactly," Glen said.

"Did you report it to the sheriff?" Jaxson asked.

"No. What could he do? Truth be told, the lithium chloride was really old. I'm not sure I could have used it anyway. Besides, the deductible from the insurance would cost more than buying it new."

He still should have told Steve about it. Otherwise, it looked like he might be involved somehow.

Jaxson looked around. "Do you have security cameras here?"

"No. The boss is too cheap."

I looked up and spotted a few. "Then what are those?"

"Fakes," Christian said.

That stunk. "If the chemical is inexpensive, why steal it and chance getting caught?"

Glen shrugged. "Maybe he didn't want anyone to know he had it."

That was a stretch. "Any guess who that might be?"

Glen looked over at Christian. "There is only one person that saw me put a bottle of it away a few weeks ago."

My heartbeat sped up. "Who?"

"Aaron Reed."

I had to laugh at that one. "He's a fireman."

"So? I graduated two years ahead of Aaron, and the guy had problems even back then," Glen said.

"I know Aaron a bit. I graduated a year after him," Jaxson said.

Glen studied Jaxson. "Sorry, bro, I don't remember you."

Jaxson shrugged. "I was trouble back then."

"So was Aaron, which is why I'm thinking he might have set the fire," Glen said.

That was ridiculous. "Aaron was the one who put it out. Why would he commit arson?"

"For people like him, the chance to be a hero is a huge draw. I know that he loved the adrenaline rush. He doesn't battle the flames because he is a good person who wants to save lives. He wants the fame and power that comes with putting out a blaze."

Ouch. Clearly, these two didn't get along. "So, you think he set the fire in order to be a hero?"

"Yes."

Wow. Sad to say, it wouldn't be the first time I'd heard of that happening. "Do you have any other reason to suspect Aaron would break into a garage, steal a chemical that he could easily buy, and then set a bookstore on fire?"

"Maybe he doesn't like to read."

I groaned. "Basically, you have squat."

"Only my gut instinct."

I turned to Christian. "Did you know Aaron?"

"I'd recognize him if I saw him, but that's all. We didn't hang in the same circles."

I wasn't sure which circles he was referring to exactly, but that was okay. They were seven years apart in age, not that it should matter. "Thank you, Glen. We'll keep Aaron in mind."

"You bet." Glen went over to a work station, picked up

some tool, and headed to a car.

Jaxson and I then thanked Christian and left. "It might be time for you to give Aaron Reed a call," I said once we'd slipped into the car.

"I plan to, but I'm wondering what information our sheriff's department has collected."

"Do you think they'd tell us?"

"We won't know until we ask."

"Before we visit Steve and Nash to see what they know, how about we grab a tea?" I suggested.

"I like it. If Steve or Nash have learned anything important, it's possible Pearl knows about it, and if Pearl knows, so will Maude."

"True, but Steve has to know his grandmother is a total gossip. I wonder if he doesn't feed her information that he wants to get out."

Jaxson glanced over at me. "I wouldn't be surprised."

"Pearl is hard of hearing so it isn't as if she overhears a lot of conversations. Besides, anything Steve wants to keep private, he can discuss in the glass enclosed soundproof room."

Jaxson started the engine and headed toward town. "You're right. I have to say it was more exciting when we believed Pearl's intel wasn't meant to be shared. Yet despite Steve's attempt to keep information from his grandmother, we somehow learn a lot when we chat with our gossip ladies."

I chuckled. "We do at that. I say we pick Maude's brain and then try to discover what the sheriff's department knows. It might not be a lot since it's too early for the arson report to have been completed."

"I agree."

Jaxson parked in front of our office, and we walked over to the tea shop. As soon as we sat down at a table, the owner came out of the back. When her gaze caught ours, Maude made a beeline in our direction. I had the sense she was looking for gossip instead of disseminating it. Having Pearl be so closed-mouthed was upsetting the balance of things.

"Nice to see you two. Terrible about Frank's fire, isn't it?"

"Totally."

She looked around and then leaned over. "Any hint as to who might have started the blaze?"

Just as I thought. "I wish I knew. We have several suspects but no proof."

"Let me get you two something to drink, and maybe we can chat."

I'd heard that line before. We ordered our usual, and she took off. When Maude returned with our drinks, she pulled up a chair. "Tell me what you've learned," she said.

I chuckled. "You're usually the one with all of the information."

"I know, but this case is different."

I could figure out why. "Because Pearl isn't being forthcoming?"

"Oh, she was forthcoming all right, only she is so sure Frank is guilty that Pearl won't consider any other options."

That matched what Dolly said. Jane's explanation of Frank not supporting Pearl after her husband's passing might have left a sour taste in her mouth. So what if he and Betty were there for Jane?

"Aunt Fern told me that Frank used to be the fire chief.

Do you know why he quit? It seemed like a job he was ideally suited for."

Maude nodded. "He was perfect for the job, but when he met Betty, she was afraid something bad would happen to him and asked him to quit. Fires scared her. She was burned in one once. Nothing serious, but it was enough to make her cautious."

I could understand that. "Would a fire chief even need to enter a burning building, though? I thought they stayed back and directed traffic, so to speak."

"Back then, the department was very small. They needed his help."

That made sense. "When Frank quit, why didn't the job go to Kevin Silver?" I asked.

Maude glanced to the side. "It would have, but right before Frank left as chief, Kevin was injured when a burning beam fell and hit him. Some say Frank shouldn't have let Kevin go inside since the building was already on the verge of collapse."

"How terrible. Did Kevin ever recover?"

"Yes, but it took months. In the meantime, someone else was offered the chief's job."

That was good information. If I were Ian Silver, I might want to get back at Frank for basically ruining my dad's shot at the top position. Because harming another was against the law, and Ian seemed like a very upstanding citizen, I couldn't imagine him doing something like that, however. Then again, I'd misjudged people in the past.

Chapter Five

AFTER WE FINISHED our tea, we walked across the street to the sheriff's office, though I wasn't very hopeful Steve would, or could, provide us with anything useful. At the very least, we could tell him what we'd found out. I figured the more help we were to him, the more likely he'd share with us.

When I spotted Pearl at the reception desk, I expected her to bombard us with bad press about Frank, but instead, she smiled sweetly and told us to head on back to Steve's office. Had she changed her mind about Frank? Or had the rumor mill exaggerated Pearl's dislike of him? I had a feeling it was the latter.

To my delight, Nash was with the sheriff.

Steve's brows rose. "Well, well. It's been what? Seven hours since the fire? I thought you'd have been here first thing this morning, Glinda." Thankfully, Steve smiled after that comment.

"For your information, Jaxson and I have been busy trying to help figure out who would have set the fire."

Nash jumped up and motioned we take the two seats. "I'll drag in another one."

I wanted to wait for him to return before giving out any information.

"I'm sorry, Glinda, I know that you care for Frank and Betty Sanchez, especially since your cousin is dating their grandson. What have you learned?" Steve now sounded totally professional.

"I'm sure you've heard the scuttlebutt about Frank setting the fire, but according to Andorra's familiar, Hugo, someone broke into the back of the bookstore."

"Yes, the lock was jimmied."

He knew, and yet he still thought Frank could be guilty? "Why would Frank jimmy a lock if he was the owner?" Or had I assumed he thought Frank was guilty, because his grandmother possibly thought that?

The sheriff stared at me for a bit. "Really? I never said Frank was guilty, but you of all people know that few things are what they seem. Many years ago, Frank was the fire chief. He'd understand exactly what it would take to divert attention away from himself."

I guess Steve did have the same target on Frank's back that his grandmother did. Maybe there was some issue I was unaware of. "It could be, but do you have any proof that he might be guilty, other than some twenty-year old grudge between him and a few others?"

"Not yet."

Good. "I assume you are aware that the pink smoke was due to lithium chloride igniting." Okay, there were probably many other chemicals that would produce the pink color, but that was my guess at the moment.

Steve's lips quirked up. "Have you been picking Ian Silver's brain now?"

"No." I'm not sure why I wasn't ready to mention that

Jaxson had done some research. "Is it true that the smoke was caused by the lithium chloride?"

"Yes."

"Do you know where Frank got the chemical?" I raised a brow. His suspicion of Frank had to have been based on something tangible.

"I never said Frank bought the chemical, but it turns out he had a box of Magic Flame packets in the storage room in the back. Those packets, when tossed in a wood fireplace, create colored flames. Some are multicolored, while others are only one color. You can guess which box of packets caught on fire and which chemical was an ingredient."

I could. "Lithium chloride, which makes the smoke turn pink."

"Exactly. Now that spring is here, no one has fires, which is why the excess packets were stored in the back room."

The question was why did Frank sell that stuff in the first place? Greeting cards, puzzles, and calendars made sense, but not fireplace stuff. Hey, maybe there had been a sale on the stuff, and Frank hoped to make an extra buck during the winter months.

"Oh." So much for that clue. It meant whoever had stolen the chemical from the garage hadn't been the arsonist. Win some, lose some. On the plus side, I would be buying some of those Magic Flames once the cold season arrived.

"Anything else?" Steve asked.

Jaxson and I told him everything we'd learned. "As you can see, there are several other viable suspects."

"Including the arson investigator. I see. That could mess up a few things if that turned out to be true," Steve said.

"Every arson case Ian ever worked on could be challenged and possibly overturned in court. If that happened, it would be a nightmare."

"I have an acquaintance over in Ocean View who is the arson investigator there," Nash said. "Should we need to check the report, we can ask him."

"Sounds good." Steve looked back over at us. "I have to say, you two have been busy. Other than Ian Silver, who is your next suspect, since you clearly don't believe Frank is guilty."

I looked over at Jaxson. "We are still working on it," I said.

"Fine, but please keep us up to date with your theories."

"We will." So far, we'd been doing all of the talking. "Do you have any suggestions where we should look?"

"Nope. Just do your best to keep the clues coming."

So much for sharing. "Thanks, and let us know if anything comes up on your end."

"Sure thing."

I doubted that. Steve was not telling us anything. Why would he change now? When we left, I was feeling rather dissatisfied. I kept quiet, though, as we headed across the street.

"Are you mad at Steve?" Jaxson asked.

I looked up at him. "Kind of. We told him about Frank's history, about Ian possibly wanting revenge, and even about how much Jane seemed to like Frank. She might have wanted to help him out by promising him the insurance money."

Jaxson scrunched his brows. "That implies Frank set the fire."

I grunted and then dragged myself up the steps to the office. "Maybe. I'm just confused. And then there is Heath Richards, yet Steve still thinks it's Frank."

"He never said that, but don't worry, the truth will come out eventually."

"I know. I'm probably upset because the lithium chloride clue was a bust."

"I understand." Jaxson rubbed my shoulder, which helped diffuse the tension.

We entered the office. "Iggy, are you here?"

When he didn't answer, I figured he was with Aimee. Good. He needed to socialize, even though he'd made a new friend with Hugo.

"How about I see if Drake is free to help us brainstorm?" Jaxson said.

His suggestion brightened my mood. "That's a great idea. We can go downstairs if he wants to keep an eye on his shop."

"I'll give him a call."

While Jaxson spoke with his brother, I grabbed some drinks. I was missing some clue, but I just couldn't put my finger on what it was. I had the sense Bertha was the key, but I didn't know how.

Jaxson poked his head in our kitchen a second before I walked out with my hands full. "Drake is having lunch with Andorra downstairs, so he asked if we could join him there. I can drag the whiteboard down there if you want."

"Perfect. I'll carry the drinks." It was always better when we could talk things out together.

Once we were set up in Drake's back room, I began my spiel. "In an effort to be fair, I will list all suspects. Like always, we need to give a number to each of them, from one to ten, that represents the likelihood that the person is the arsonist." I also had a column for why we thought the person could be guilty.

Jaxson detailed what we'd learned while I tried to summarize our findings on the board. "Who do you think is the arsonist?" I hope they didn't say Frank.

"I'm voting for Heath Richards," Andorra said.

That didn't surprise me since her store had a lot to lose if he was the culprit. "Tell us why."

"He has the most to gain financially by burning down the store. Frank's insurance would cover the interior items, and Heath's would take care of any structural damage. Unless Frank chose to restock, Heath could rent to someone new. I did some checking and learned that Frank, my grandmother, as well as Silas and Kathy Adams, are the only three stores left that pay next to nothing for rent."

I wrote that on the board. "If Heath Richards is guilty, that is scary. I hope Bertha plans to put in security cameras."

Andorra nodded. "She promised to."

"Good."

"Oh," Andorra said. "In passing, I learned something. According to my friend Silvia, Terry Alden used to date Glen Harmony."

"Why is that important? Glen isn't a suspect," I said.

"Maybe not, but he did accuse Aaron of stealing something that we believed at the time was used in the fire," Andorra said.

"I'm not following."

"Apparently, Aaron Reed started hanging around Terry,

and eventually, Terry left Glen to be with Aaron."

I waited to hear the bad part, but something wasn't fitting. "People date around. Why is that malicious?"

"Turns out Glen and Aaron have a history of not liking each other, though I wasn't able to find out why," Andorra said.

Drake munched on a cracker. "Is it possible Glen set the fire in order to set up Aaron for stealing his girlfriend?" When no one answered, he continued. "Glen might have spotted the packets of Magic Flames when he was in the bookstore's back room getting ready to set the place on fire. He recognized what chemicals were used to make the colored flames, and then thought of the perfect way to frame Aaron."

I had to think about that. "Glen was quite convincing that Aaron was the thief."

Drake shook his head. "On second thought, Glen couldn't have known that Aaron would even be working that night."

"I don't think that matters," I said. "Glen might have thought the pink smoke would lead us or the sheriff to the garage where he works, allowing him to point the finger at Aaron. It wouldn't matter if Aaron was on duty or not."

Jaxson held up a hand. "Except that even Christian knew that chemical was used in a variety of places. We got lucky in learning that Glen used it. We now know that lithium chloride in its raw form wasn't even used in the fire. If Glen was the arsonist, he'd have picked something better."

"I disagree. He might have believed the arson investigator wouldn't notice the Magic Flames, especially if they burned up."

"I still think if he knew those magic colored packets had caught fire, he would have found something better to frame Aaron with," Jaxson said.

Andorra grunted. "Just put Glen on the list and move on. From what Drake told me, sometimes it is the person you least expect who turns out to be the guilty party."

I huffed out a laugh. "You are so right. After Jaxson was accused of killing our deputy, I didn't have a clue about the real killer until she made a mistake." I wrote down Glen's name. "It would be nice to get confirmation from Aaron about this dislike and the possible theft."

"I was planning on chatting with him today," Jaxson said. "I'll ask if he was even at Cove Garage recently, not that it really matters now, but it might get him talking about Glen and their beef."

Drake held up his hands. "Guys, Andi's right. We need to move on. Let's continue assigning numbers for the rest of the people."

He was such a good influence on us. "Fine. We'll give Glen a one. I say, Aaron should be given a five."

When everyone agreed, I marked it down. We then went through the rest of the list. I had to admit I was happy no new names—other than Glen's—had been added. We had enough on our hands.

Eventually, Andorra had to go back to work, as did Drake, so Jaxson carried our whiteboard upstairs. When we reached the office, Iggy was there.

"Hey, there, buddy. How was Aimee?" Jaxson asked as he set down the whiteboard.

"Good."

My familiar didn't sound happy. "What's going on, Iggy?"

"Nothing." He disappeared under the sofa.

When he got in that mood, it was best to leave him alone. He'd tell us what was bothering him eventually. I hope Aimee hadn't snubbed him again. Cats were rather fickle animals.

"I'm going to see what I can find out at the fire station," Jaxson said.

"Do you think Aaron will be there? He was working late last night putting out the fire." Though it appeared as if the sprinkler system did most of the work.

"If he's not there, I'm sure I can find out where he lives and talk to him at his house." He leaned over and kissed me. "Wish me luck."

"Good luck."

Jaxson seemed happy to be the one who knew the suspect for a change. Once he left, though, I was at a loss for what to do next. It was only when I spotted a book I'd purchased from the bookstore a while ago that reminded me I needed to speak with Frank. The problem was that he wouldn't be at his store, and I didn't know where he lived. However, there was at least one person who would know his location: Gavin Sanchez, his grandson, who should be with his mother at the morgue.

Elissa Sanchez was Frank's daughter-in-law, but from what I'd gleaned, they hadn't been close since she and Frank's son, Daniel, had divorced a long time ago. After Gavin's father's death, however, Elissa and Frank had grown a bit closer. I was hoping she or her son could give me some information about the fire—and also tell me where Frank lived. I should know, but I never had the occasion to visit him and Betty at their house. They pretty much kept to themselves.

I bent over and spotted Iggy's tail under the sofa. "I'm going to talk to Dr. Sanchez and Gavin at the morgue."

"I'll stay here. The morgue stinks. Remember you promised that when you went there, you'd take some perfume with you."

He always thought I smelled bad when I returned home. "Can do, but I'll have to stop by my apartment before I come back here then."

"Works for me."

I chuckled at his antics. Because it was nice out, I walked to the morgue. To my surprise, Elissa was in the main office area instead of in the *smelly* autopsy room.

She looked up and smiled. "Glinda, this is a surprise."

Was it really? She had to know I'd be investigating the fire. "Do you have a minute to talk?"

Just then Gavin came out of the back. "Hey, Glinda. I thought I heard your voice."

"Good, you're here. I was hoping to chat with you two about your grandfather."

"Poor grandpa. He's such a mess."

That was one more reason to believe Frank hadn't set the fire. "I'm sorry. Did Frank mention who he thought might have caused the blaze?"

Elissa glanced over at her son and then back at me. "No, but if Daniel was to be believed, Frank had some enemies. That was a long time ago, though."

"Who were they?"

"It wouldn't be fair to say," she said. "As I said, it was a long time ago."

I could respect that. Besides, I probably could guess who they were. "What's going to happen to him and Betty now? Financially, I mean."

"The insurance will cover almost all of the damage, but I don't think they will start up the store again. The bookstore was Betty's idea in the first place. Since her arthritis is giving her such problems, they'll most likely retire."

"Grandpa has some issues, too."

"I'm sorry to hear that. What will they do? Sit around and watch television all day? That doesn't sound like them."

"I don't think Frank has had the chance to give it much thought. Betty is his main concern now."

"That's nice, but can they afford not to work?" Sure, I was asking personal questions, but I believed it might have a bearing on the case.

"Actually, they can," Elissa said. "The insurance money will help, but when Daniel died, he left them money."

I had no idea. There goes my aunt's theory that Frank had to set his place on fire because he needed the insurance money. "That's great. I imagine Heath Richards will be happy. Now he can charge more rent when he gets a new tenant."

Elissa chuckled. "Heath is a business man. His dad was not."

That implied she didn't think ill of him. Interesting. "What can you tell me about Frank's and Ian Silver's dad's past interactions?"

Chapter Six

"T HAT WAS BEFORE my time," Elissa said.

I should have thought of that. Elissa only moved here a few years ago.

"Dad talked about it once. He told me that Grandpa felt real bad about the way he was selected as fire chief," Gavin said.

"How so?" I was curious to learn another take on what happened—assuming there was more than one version.

"He got the job only because some other guy was injured in a fire."

"I might feel a little guilty, too." I didn't dare suggest a different side of the story about Kevin Silver's injuries—that he'd been hurt after Frank became chief. I turned back to Gavin's mom. "Did Frank call you today when he found out about the fire?"

"Actually, Nash called and told me what happened," she said.

"Have you spoken with them?"

"Yes, but we only talked for a minute. Frank was trying to calm Betty down. I'd never heard him so upset."

Perhaps my plan to chat with him today should wait. He needed time to deal with what happened. "I'll stop over in a few days to offer my condolences, but believe it or not, I don't know where Frank lives."

Elissa smiled. "Or do you really want to ask about who might have set the fire?"

Why did everyone think I only had a one-track mind? Yes, I was focused as an investigator, but I cared about the Sanchezes. "First and foremost, I want to make sure they are okay. If I am able to help find out who did this, all the better." I held up a hand. "I know Nash and Steve will do everything possible to solve this case quickly, but Bertha had a feeling that more than just an ordinary arsonist was involved."

I know, I know. She never said that directly, but magic could have been used, and her gut feelings should not be dismissed. Bertha was a talented witch.

"Are we talking magic?"

Magic had been involved in the last few cases I'd worked on. "I have no evidence that indicates it, but I need to be open to all possibilities."

"I don't think either of my grandparents believe in that stuff even though they live in Witch's Cove."

"I know, but I think witches and warlocks—at least the bad ones—don't want anyone to believe in them. It's how they hope to get away with things."

Elissa pulled out her phone and typed in something. "I just sent you their address and phone number, but please give them a call before you go over."

"Absolutely. If you learn anything, call me, okay?"

Elissa hugged me. "Thank you for taking such good care of our town."

"Of course."

I left, but I wasn't sure I'd learned a whole lot other than where Frank lived and the fact he would be okay financially. That part made me feel better.

I wasn't back at the office more than twenty minutes when Jaxson returned. I couldn't tell from his expression whether he had been successful finding Aaron or not.

"So?" I asked.

"I spoke with Aaron. It was a little awkward at first. I don't think he liked having people around who knew him when he was in high school."

"I can understand that since you said he was kind of a thug. Being this big fireman, I wouldn't want my past to define me. Of all people, you should understand that."

Jaxson nodded. "I do. How about I grab us some drinks, and we can chat?"

"I like that idea."

Jaxson came back a moment later with my sweet tea and a mug of coffee for himself. As soon as he set them on the table and sat down, Iggy jumped on his lap. It did my heart good to see those two bond.

"What did Aaron say?" I asked.

"He didn't know who called in the fire. He'd just arrived to work when the bell rang that signified the truck was needed. It's what the men live for."

"Is it possible Aaron could have set the fire himself and then hustled back to the station?"

"I'm not discounting anything or anyone," Jaxson said. "I know I mentioned magic, but I don't recall Aaron being a warlock."

"When I was in high school, a lot of kids kept their talents secret. No one wanted to be different. We all just wanted to fit in."

Jaxson picked up his mug and sipped the hot brew. "You might be right."

"Did you ask him what started the fire?"

"I did. He rushed to where the pink smoke was coming from and then found remnants of the packages containing the Magic Flames. That wasn't what started the fire, however."

"Was it an accelerant?"

"He didn't know, but he hoped the arson investigator would figure it out."

I have never studied fire theory, but I've seen enough crime shows to know firemen could at least identify a pour pattern. Then again, that could be television drama stuff.

"Did you ask him why Glen would accuse him of stealing the chemical in the garage locker?"

Jaxson held up a hand. "Yes, I'm getting to that. Aaron was very forthcoming about being at the garage. He needed to get his car fixed. When he brought it in, he spotted Glen with the chemical. Aaron said that Glen's claim is totally bogus. Aaron never returned to the garage, so he didn't steal anything. He believes that Glen is angry because of losing Terry."

"Nothing else? No old grudge?"

"I didn't ask, but there certainly could have been bad blood over something years ago. Aaron was trouble back then."

"So Glen says. It makes sense. Did you ask him why he chose to be a fireman?" I'd mentioned to Jaxson that I didn't buy Glen's claim of Aaron being in search of fame.

"As a matter of fact, I did. You'd be proud of how I slipped that in a question. Turns out when Aaron was eight, his mother fell asleep in a lounge chair smoking a cigarette.

When she caught fire, she screamed, which woke up her young son."

I hissed in a breath. "That is so horrible. Did he see it?"

"I'm afraid so. Aaron tried to save her, but he couldn't. It's what made him want to become a fireman."

"Where was the dad?"

"He worked some late shift at a factory."

"I can't imagine." I shivered at the thought. Poor Aaron. Glen had been so wrong about him.

Jaxson cleared his throat. "What's next on the agenda?"

"Good question. I know we haven't learned the cause of the fire, but if magic is involved, I'd like to know if someone can light a fire by using a spell."

"Sounds like a good place to start. Are you going to ask Levy?"

"Yes, in part because Bertha doesn't know if it's possible. I'd bug Gertrude, but Levy and his coven have that extensive library and a lot of people willing to comb through the books."

"Do you want me to come with you?" he asked.

I sucked in a breath. "I kind of promised Bertha that I would take her."

Jaxson held up a hand. "By all means. I'm sure I can find something to occupy my time."

"You are the best."

"Just come back with how to light a fire with your mind. If we go camping, I won't have to carry a lighter." He winked.

I laughed. "I'm not sure it works that way." Actually, I had no idea how it worked. "Let me call Levy and see if he and his team are even free to meet with us."

Thankfully, my go-to warlock worked from home. Otherwise, taking off whenever he chose would have been difficult. I dialed his number.

"Glinda! I haven't heard from you in a while. What's up?"

I told him about the bookstore burning down.

"My grandmother mentioned that happened. It's so terrible. Do you have any suspects?"

"Too many, but Bertha, who runs the Hex and Bones—"

"I know Bertha. She's talented."

I smiled. "She is." I explained who we thought might be guilty. "I know this sounds crazy, but I'm wondering if magic is involved. The fireman—one of our suspects—said he couldn't tell how the fire started. Either he is lying, is incompetent, or someone started it with magic. Have you ever heard of a witch or warlock being able to light a fire using a spell?"

Levy said nothing for a moment. "No, but that doesn't mean it can't be done. I can gather a few of the members and ask them to do a little research. It will make their day. Can you meet us, say in an hour, at the library?"

I mentally pumped a fist. "Yes. Would it be all right if Bertha came? She's really excited to see your collection."

"Of course. We'd love to have her."

For the first time since I spotted the pink smoke, I was filled with hope. "See you soon." I hung up and faced Jaxson. "He said yes."

Jaxson chuckled. "I figured. Even if you learn the spell, how will that narrow the field? Other than Christian, who I'm pretty sure is not involved, no one has powers."

"That we know of. But first things first. If we understand this person's abilities, we might be able to identify him or her."

"Good thinking."

I called Bertha to invite her to visit Levy and his coven at their amazing library. Needless to say, she was ecstatic. Once Andorra and Elizabeth assured her they'd cover for her, she told me she'd be ready when I was.

"See you in forty-five minutes."

"Perfect."

I hung up and turned to Jaxson. "What are you going to do now?"

"If I knew Ian Silver better, I'd sniff around to see what he thinks caused the fire."

"If you tell him you're investigating the blaze, maybe he'll give you a clue even though it is still early. He would be a good person to get to know better, right?"

Jaxson chuckled. "You are something else. Sure, why not. I'll give him a call. The worst that can happen is he'll say he's too busy to talk."

Iggy looked up at me. "Do you want to come with me and Bertha to see Levy?" I asked.

He lifted his chest. "Yes!"

Maybe his malaise had been due to inactivity. When we were at the library, everyone would be able to understand him, which would be a pleasant change for my familiar.

When it was time to go, Iggy hopped in my purse, and we took off. Since the library where Levy's coven met was two towns over, I had to drive. I parked in front of the Hex and Bones, because I had to pick up Bertha. I went into the store, happy to see she was ready.

"I can't believe I'm going to see this amazing archive. I've never been in a coven library before."

"I was rather intimidated the first time I was there, but

once I got to know the people, I found them warm and friendly."

"I can't wait." Once in the car, Bertha twisted toward me. "Tell me about these coven members."

I gave her the rundown of who was who. "There are a lot of members I've yet to meet. No telling who will be free to search through the books for the spell we're trying to find."

"Not that I have any experience in creating fire, but if I were to burn down a building, having to say a spell using herbs and stuff seems impractical."

"I agree, but what else is there? I doubt dragons exist, though I never would have believed a stone gargoyle statue could change into a living human either."

Bertha smiled. "There you go."

When we arrived, I didn't see Levy or any of his coven members anywhere. "Maybe we're early."

We both exited the car and walked up to the door that had no handle. I knocked.

"How can one get inside?" Bertha asked.

I pointed to the eye scanner and fingerprint pad. "It's very high tech."

"I can see that."

A moment later, the door opened, and Levy, our very powerful warlock, greeted us.

"Sorry. I got wrapped up in looking for the spell. Come in."

Bertha walked slowly down the darkened hallway, probably because she was studying the rather strange surroundings. When we arrived at the main room, I faced her. "Be prepared to be impressed."

She giggled, acting one fourth of her age. "I can't wait."

Chapter Seven

A S SOON AS we stepped into the room lined with books, Bertha halted and sucked in a breath. "Are these all magic books?"

I smiled. I loved seeing her so excited. "They are."

Levy introduced her to the three members present. I recognized two of them. One was Camila, a werewolf-witch hybrid, one was Diego, and the third turned out to be relatively new member named Dax.

Iggy popped his head out and looked around. "It smells old in here."

Everyone laughed. Camila stood up and came over to my familiar. "He is adorable."

"Thank you, but I think he'd prefer it if you thought he looked intelligent."

She lifted up his collar. "Detective Iggy. Impressive. Can you read?"

Iggy looked back and me, and I immediately pressed lightly on his mouth. I knew he was about to say something snarky. "Why yes he can. Turning the pages is a bit more difficult, but I'll let him help you if you want."

"That would be great, if it's okay with Iggy."

I released my hold, allowing him to answer. "Yes!" Iggy

then jumped out of my grasp and scooted across the table to Camila.

"Traitor," I said.

"You get to bask in my brilliance all the time," he shot back.

I didn't want to argue. "I do."

Once Iggy was situated next to his new friend, Levy looked from Diego to Camila to Dax. "What have you found, gang?"

Camila sighed. "Just two spells that can make a rock glow. No fire yet."

"That's a possibility. Does it say if the rock can get hot enough to set a piece of paper on fire? The bookstore was full of flammable items." I explained about the packets of colored smoke catching on fire. Once more I questioned the reason he had them, but since they didn't start the fire, I suppose it didn't really matter.

"It could," Camila said. "I think we can do better though. Fire has been with us for thousands of years, as have witches. Surely, some have been able to harness its power."

That was what I was hoping. Levy motioned we take a seat. He then grabbed a few books from the other end of the table and slid them in front of us. I had to guess his coven had narrowed it down to these tomes. There weren't many markings on the shelves to show where things were, but they probably knew. Maybe that was one of their skills.

"Start searching, ladies," he said, as he took a book for himself.

My problem was that I wanted to read each and every spell. My witch abilities were growing, but my knowledge of what a warlock could do was still limited. After this case, I should ask to come here just to study.

Bertha already had her nose in the book. Her eyes would grow wide and then narrow as she poured over the information. If I knew what I was looking for, it would make things easier.

After twenty minutes of us looking over the books in silence, I located something that appeared promising until I read the details. It involved several people of magic saying a spell together. Both Levy's coven and my little collection of witches had performed group spells. Without a doubt they had been effective, but in this case it wouldn't have been practical.

"I might have something," Levy said. "It's probably not what you want, but I think it could work."

We all looked up. "What is it?"

"Fire itself isn't created, but there is lots of heat."

"Enough to set paper on fire?"

He ran his finger across the page. "It doesn't say exactly."

"How does it work? Is there a spell involved?"

"That's the strange part. No, there isn't. Actually, what is even odder is that someone reported seeing an angry woman touch someone. The mere contact burned that person."

"Ouch. No fire?"

"No, but it doesn't say whether it could set something on fire."

"I would think if it burned skin, it might burn paper," I added.

"Let's not rule anything out. Keep looking, people."

As I searched through the books, I tried to rifle through

my memory for anyone who had a hot handshake or who had been burned by the human touch, but I came up empty.

"I got something," Diego called. "A witch or warlock can recreate fire, but it takes a lengthy spell."

"We never said the arsonist was in and out in seconds," I said.

"I know, but there are several ingredients here that you can't even get in the United States. Yak hair? Sap from a bansmil tree? I've never even heard of that kind of plant."

I looked over at Bertha, but she shrugged.

"With the ingredients and the lengthy spell, the witch could start a fire, right?" I asked.

"In theory, yes," he said.

"That gives me hope then." We spent another hour searching. With each minute that passed, my guilt grew. I hated to keep everyone on what might be a wild goose chase. "I think I might go the non-magic route for now. Not all crimes involve people with magical abilities."

Levy chuckled. "True, but don't rule it out. I'll see if I can ask some others to check out different sources."

"Thank you." I pushed back my chair and then helped Bertha up.

Levy escorted us out, and I thanked him again. Once we returned to the car, Bertha remained rather quiet as I started the engine and headed out. "What's wrong?" I asked her.

"It's so strange. When I arrived at work this morning, I smelled the smoke, but I also had this sense of heat."

"Fire causes heat." I realize that was an obvious statement.

"I know, but it was more than that. I didn't mention anything before, but I could almost feel anger and heat swirling in the Hex and Bones store."

That was interesting. "What time did you get to work?"

She shrugged. "At nine. My usual time. Why?"

"The fire happened a little before four in the morning, which means you arrived at work five hours after the blaze. Would you feel any vibes from the arsonist after that much time had passed?" I had no idea how that worked.

"I don't know, but this is the first time I've felt something like this. It was different from what I'd sensed before, which is why I didn't say for sure magic was involved. But when Levy read about the heat and the anger, it resonated with me."

"Great. We're getting somewhere. Now all we need to do is find someone with a temper and a grudge against Frank."

Bertha placed a hand on my arm. "You are funny, Glinda. I know it sounds impossible, but something will reveal itself to us."

She really did sound like Jaxson. "Let's hope. I wonder if the anger has to be real or if the warlock can concentrate hard to make himself mad."

"Excellent question."

She was no help. "Even if we knew the answer, it doesn't point a finger at a specific person."

"No, it doesn't."

When I pulled in front of the store, Iggy asked if he could say hi to Hugo. "Sure."

I hadn't planned my next move anyway even though Levy and his coven had provided me with some answers. As soon as we went inside, Iggy crawled out of my purse, raced down my leg, and darted across the floor.

Bertha stopped and grabbed my arm. "That's Heath

Richards. I hope he's not here to inspect the place."

"Let him," I said. "The store looks great."

"Men like him will find the smallest thing wrong so they can kick us out or make us pay triple the rent."

"Let's hope he's here merely to see there was no fire damage."

"Let's hope."

As much as I wanted to listen in, I needed to let them talk in private. I'd ask Andorra later about the visit, unless she already knew why the building owner was there.

My friend smiled as I neared. "How did it go?" she asked.

"Okay, I guess. Nothing definitive." I explained that the closest thing to a fire was the existence of some witches being able to heat up their bodies—or maybe it was their hands—so much so that it could burn skin. "I thought that amount of heat might set paper on fire."

Her mouth opened. "Someone can touch another person and burn them?"

Something was going on. "Yes, why?"

"This might mean nothing, but when I was talking to Sylvia, the one who is friends with Terry Alden, she said that Terry had been burned a few months ago."

"By what?"

"That's the thing. She doesn't remember. The next day, these blisters showed up on her arm."

That was strange. "Do you think we could talk to Terry?"

"I guess. She works at the library."

Awesome. "Delilah Smithson works there, too."

"Really? I remember her. Sweet, sweet girl."

"Yes, she is. The library is open until eight. How about

you, me, Drake, and Jaxson grab an early dinner and then head on over there," I suggested.

"I'll see if Drake is free, and then I'll call over to see if Terry is working tonight."

"Sounds like a plan." I nodded to Heath Richards. "What's the owner doing here?"

"He said he wanted to make sure the fire didn't damage yet another one of his stores." She inhaled deeply.

"I hear a *but* coming?" She must think he had an ulterior motive.

"I don't know. Did he come to see if Memaw was afraid the same thing would happen to her? Or does he want to find something amiss so he can evict her?"

I studied him. He was about thirty-five and rather good looking. "I wish I could tell if he has powers."

"I'll ask Hugo after Mr. Richards leaves. While Hugo can't say for sure, he has these hunches sometimes that seem to be rather accurate."

"Good to know. Maybe Iggy can pry something out of Hugo's memory."

Andorra smiled. "Maybe." She pulled out her phone. "I'll give the library a call to see if Terry is working tonight, and then I'll ask Drake if he can join us for dinner."

"Great."

I would have left right away to see what Jaxson had uncovered after speaking with Ian Silver, but I wanted to give Iggy time to chat with Hugo. I had no idea what those two were discussing.

After Andorra made her calls, she reported back. "Everything is set. How about the Tiki Hut at five thirty?"

"Works for me."

I went into the back room and found Iggy sitting on Hugo's lap. I had to smile. "Hey there. We have to go."

"Already? I was just telling Hugo about the room with all of the magic books."

I was curious if Hugo knew how to read. If he'd been a statue his whole life, I couldn't imagine he'd have had the time to study. "Great. We can come back at another time."

He lowered his head. "Okay."

I snapped my fingers. "You know, Andorra is meeting Jaxson and me for dinner at five thirty. Do you want her to take you later?"

"Yes!"

"Okay then." I assumed she'd be okay with it.

On my way out, I spoke with her about taking Iggy when she met us for dinner. "I'd be happy to."

"Thanks."

We hugged goodbye. Bertha was still with Mr. Richards, and since I didn't want to disturb her, I left. I drove across the street to the Tiki Hut and then went next door to our office.

Jaxson was hunched over the computer. "Hey," I said.

He turned around and smiled. "How did it go?"

I detailed what Bertha and I had and hadn't found. "When I dropped her off at the Hex and Bones, you'll never guess who was there."

"Hugo."

"Well, yes. Hugo is always there. This time it was Heath Richards."

Jaxson looked like he'd seen a ghost. "That's not good."

"What do you mean?"

Chapter Eight

"I'VE BEEN DOING research on our building owner." Jaxson pressed his lips together.

That didn't sound good. "What did you find?"

"He's not in good shape financially. His father's business acumen—or lack of it—has seriously put the family in debt."

I hated to hear that. "I know Heath Richards owns the building across the street, but what else does he own?"

"That was a bit harder to find out, but I discovered that he owns two strip malls in Summertime and one in Palm Ridge. There could be more, but I'd have to check courthouse records to be sure. I think he just closed one of the malls in Summertime."

"He didn't try to sell it?"

Jaxson shrugged. "I imagine he will try, but it would take time for all of the owners to leave. If I were him, I'd spend some money sprucing up the place first."

"Ouch. I hope Heath Richards isn't planning on closing down the one here. Whoever purchased it might not abide by Ben Richard's rent policy."

"Exactly."

I held up a finger. "I almost forgot. You were going to meet with the arson investigator. How did that go?"

He tapped the chair next to him, and I sat down. "Not as well as I'd hoped, but it was interesting. Naturally, he's not allowed to disclose any information about the fire—especially since it happened last night."

"From the slight twinkle in your eye, would it be fair to say he broke his rule?"

"He did, but I think it's because he's frustrated. Believe it or not, he is aware of the Pink Iguana Sleuths and our success rate." Jaxson brushed his knuckles across his chest.

"That's great. Does he know we are kind of good with magic stuff?"

"Yes, which was why he was willing to speak with me."

"Tell me."

"There was no accelerant."

"That would support the magic theory. Or isn't he open to that weird witch stuff?"

"Ian seems to be open-minded. Here's the strange thing. The fire started in multiple places, almost as if the person walked around the room and lit a match to thirty different books."

I had to think about that. "That's odd."

"Yes. Ian has never seen that happen, which opened his mind to alternative ideas."

"Did he come up with the magic concept by himself?"

"This is Witch's Cove. Ian recognized that a match alone wouldn't do the trick. It would have to be something bigger and more powerful."

"How about if the person used a blow torch?" I asked.

"He and his team are working on that concept, but Ian says the scorch marks are unlike anything he's seen. Whoever did it was able to basically destroy a lot of books at once. Had it not been for his team getting there so fast, the fire might have spread to other stores—fire walls or no fire walls."

"Yikes."

"I know."

"Did you ask who called in the fire?" I asked.

"I did. It was some waitress working the late shift. She was cutting through town when she spotted the smoke and called 911."

So much for the arsonist wanting us to stop the fire from spreading, as Jaxson had suggested. I turned back to him. "What will Ian put in his arson report? I'm hoping he won't say the fire was due to faulty wiring or something."

"No. Ian is convinced it is arson, but he needs to have a plausible explanation for how the fire started. Saying it was magic isn't going to work."

"I get it. Did Ian ask for our help by any chance?"

"Yes and no. He couldn't come out and ask directly, but I think he'd welcome any input."

I smiled. "Great."

"Is Levy going to continue looking for a fire spell?" he asked.

"Yes, but he didn't sound hopeful. Could someone go around touching a bunch of books and have then catch fire at once? Who's to say, but if the arsonist is mad enough, maybe. For all I know, his anger could radiate out of his fingertips and set multiple books on fire at once."

"So, nothing definitive."

"No, but we will find out tonight what Bertha and Mr. Richards discussed, assuming you are up for dinner with

Andorra and your brother. And Iggy. That might lead us in the right direction."

He grinned. "I'd love to do dinner."

The door to the office opened, and my cousin, Rihanna, came in. "Hey, how was school?" I asked.

She always answered the same, but I wanted her to know that I cared. I was nine years older, but I felt like her mom, even though her actual mother was back in Jacksonville, Florida, and doing wonderfully after completing rehab.

"Good, but it was strange."

That was different. "Strange how?"

"You know the fire at the bookstore?" She slipped off her backpack and tossed it on the sofa.

"Yes."

She grinned. "I figured you two would be working on it all day. Well, at lunch today, this kid announces that *he* set the fire last night."

Without thinking, I reached out and grabbed Jaxson's shoulder. "For real?"

"Yes, for real, but I don't think he did it."

That was a bit disappointing, though having a high school kid be guilty wouldn't have sat well with me. "Because?"

She tilted her head. "I talked to him about it."

"And you read his mind." What was I thinking? "Of course, you did." I adored my witchy cousin.

"Yes."

"If he's not guilty, why tell us, unless you think it's relevant somehow?"

She grinned. "Just in case you have no clues, this might give you hope."

I chuckled. "Hope? I don't plan on pinning it on a kid. Did he say why he set the building on fire, not that it matters if he is innocent?"

"Wilt just said the building owner deserved to pay."

I stilled. "The building owner?"

"Yes, why?" Rihanna came over to our desk area.

Jaxson explained how Heath Richards had already closed one strip mall in Summertime and that he spoke with Bertha today.

Rihanna looked a little confused. "I don't get it."

"Maybe this Wilt kid knows something about the fire. What's his last name?" I wasn't sure why I asked since I didn't know many of the kids in her school.

"Harmony."

Had I not been sitting down, my legs would have collapsed. Harmony? That wasn't a real common name. "You wouldn't know if he has a brother Glen, do you?"

"I don't know. This may sound bad, but Wilt and I don't hang in the same circles."

"Because he isn't a warlock?"

"No, silly. He has no social skills. That's all."

"Oh." I waited for Jaxson to come up with a plan, but he said nothing. "Andorra, Drake, Iggy, myself, and Jaxson are going out to dinner to discuss our next step, and I hope you'll join us."

"I'd love to. What's this big plan of yours?"

I pushed back my chair. "Let's get comfortable, and I'll fill you in on everything."

"Perfect."

While I grabbed some drinks, Rihanna changed. When

she returned, Jaxson and I gave her a blow-by-blow of our day.

"What are you thinking?" she asked.

I looked over at Jaxson, hoping he'd draw some conclusion. "We think magic is involved, and I got the sense the arson investigator agrees," he said.

"That's a start."

I nodded. "The fact that Levy found some evidence that a warlock could start a fire without a spell is encouraging."

"Do you want me to have a chat with Wilt?" she asked.

"Tomorrow is Saturday."

"Darn. Then Monday, I'll touch base and ask him why he spread that rumor."

"The only reason someone would confess to a crime was if they either did the deed or if they were trying to cover up for someone," Jaxson said.

My brows pinched. "Garage mechanic Glen is now a suspect? We'd given him a one rating."

He shrugged. "Wilt could have broken into the garage and stolen the lithium chloride—not Aaron. I doubt Aaron is guilty, but who knows?"

Rihanna shook her head. "Again, I don't want to speak ill of people, but I don't think Wilt has it upstairs enough to even know that lithium chloride, when ignited, turns flames pink."

"Unless he thought it could be a fire starter," Jaxson said. "But I should check it out."

"Remember, the only lithium chloride that the fire department found came from the packets," I said.

"True." Jaxson went over to the computer. It took less

than a minute before he returned. "That chemical in and of itself is not combustible. It will, however, enhance the combustion of other substances."

"If Jaxson had to look it up, Wilt probably wasn't the one who took the stuff from the garage," I said. "I'm betting Glen made it up to get back at Aaron." We were going around in circles. I looked at my watch. "We should go, people. I'm hoping that Bertha's discussion with Heath Richards will point us in the right direction. She was talking with him for quite some time."

Rihanna stood. "Sounds good."

We walked over to the Tiki Hut Grill and found Iggy with my aunt at the counter while the others were seated.

While Jaxson and Rihanna sat down, I went over to my familiar. "Did you have a good time with Hugo?"

"I did."

I waited for him to add some major revelation, but he remained quiet. "Did Hugo say anything important?" I prodded.

"Just that he could sense Bertha's stress when that man came in."

"Heath Richards. He owns the building. So, nothing else?"

"Not that I can remember."

Iggy's poor memory was his biggest flaw. "I need to order. I'm sure you'll be in good hands with Aunt Fern."

"Yeah. See ya."

So much for him missing me. I returned to the table, anxious to hear what Heath Richards told Bertha. "What did I miss?"

"I know I was the one who suspected Mr. Richards of being the arsonist, but he was begging my aunt to let him raise the rent a bit. If she doesn't, he may have to sell the building," Andorra said.

I sucked in a breath. "Because he's going bankrupt?"

"I'm afraid so."

I doubted just raising Bertha's rent would do the trick. "Wow. Can anyone think of a reason why he'd be the arsonist or hire someone to torch the bookstore?" I asked.

"Nope. Do we know if Mr. Richards ever approached Frank about upping the rent?" Drake asked.

I shook my head. "I'm giving Frank some time before I bother him."

"Good idea," Jaxson said.

"Did Rihanna tell you both about Glen Harmony's brother confessing to being the arsonist?"

Drake nodded. "That is totally crazy."

"I know, but since Rihanna is pretty sure he's innocent, maybe we should increase Glen's rating."

"Definitely," Andorra said. "Every time more evidence comes in, we'll need to reevaluate our suspects."

The server came over, and after Andorra and Drake checked the menu, we all ordered. Of course, I knew what I wanted.

"I've been trying to think why Glen's little brother would confess," Jaxson said. "Let's assume he believes that Glen is guilty, even though I doubt Glen would admit it to him."

Rihanna placed the napkin on her lap. "You're right. Wilt is kind of a fragile kid. There has to be a reason why he thought his brother did it."

Jaxson leaned forward. "I have an idea, but we'll need Steve's help."

"With?" I asked.

"Do we have any idea what Glen and Wilt's parents do for a living?" he asked.

"Why would we know?" I shot back.

We all looked at Rihanna. "Don't ask me. I've barely said two words to Wilt before today."

"What if one of their parents was affected by one of the Richards' buildings shutting down? The loss of income could put the family in a tailspin," he said.

"Good thinking, bro. I bet Wilt's school would have all of that information." Drake's eyes brightened. "Hence the need to involve Sheriff Rocker. He can call the school and ask for the information."

Jaxson pointed a finger at Drake. "You got it."

"Let's say we learn that one or both parents lost their job due to the building closing," I said. "Does that mean Glen is our arsonist? For that to be true—at least for me—I'd have to know that he has magical abilities."

No one responded. Our food and drinks arrived, and we all seemed fixated on eating. Most likely, our minds were spinning too fast to talk.

"I have it," Rihanna said.

"Great! What is it?" I asked.

"If we knew who was either a witch or a warlock, it would make our search easier, right?"

"Sure," Andorra said. "How do we do that?"

My cousin smiled. "Easy. We use Iggy."

Chapter Nine

WE'D USED IGGY a few times before for sting operations, and he'd never let us down, but eventually our luck would run out. Not only that, but I didn't like exposing my familiar to danger. "Care to explain?"

"I would first ask Casi if she thinks Christian would be willing to help," Rihanna said.

Casi was not only Rihanna's new witch friend, but she was Christian's sister. "You want to use Christian in another sting operation?"

"Yes. Why not? He did great the last time."

Christian had played his part perfectly in bringing down a killer. "Okay, let's say he is willing to help. How does this work? And what part does Iggy play?"

"I haven't been involved in the picking of possible arsonists, but let's say we think Glen Harmony is guilty." She held up a hand. "I'm not saying he is. We need to start with someone."

"I'm good with that. Go on," I said.

"All I'm interested in is in determining who has magical abilities and who doesn't. We know Christian is a warlock, but we don't think he's involved in setting the fire, right?"

"Right," Jaxson said.

"Here is how it could work. We put Iggy in some kind of backpack and then ask Christian, or whoever, to carry him into the shop. If Glen is there, Iggy will cloak himself, walk up behind Glen, and say hello."

I smiled at her innovative mind. "Whenever anyone says hello behind my back, I turn around. The test will be to see if Glen turns around at the sound of Iggy's voice. If he does, we'll know he heard him, meaning he is a warlock."

Drake whistled. "I am impressed, young lady."

"Thank you. As I said, even if Glen can do magic, it doesn't mean he is guilty of arson."

"I agree. What should Iggy do then?" I asked.

"Either he'll crawl into the backpack, and Christian will find some reason to carry him outside, or Iggy will head outside where we will be there to retrieve him—once he uncloaks himself."

"I like it," Andorra said. "Whether Glen is or isn't a warlock, we have to test all of our suspects."

"Agreed. You said several people suspect Frank, right?" Rihanna asked.

"Sad to say, yes."

"I can ask Gavin to take Iggy over to visit his grandfather and have Iggy do the same thing."

"I can do it," I said. "I need to see if Frank and Betty are doing okay. While there, I can ask some questions. Bertha said Frank had spoken with Heath Richards. I'd like to know what was said, like whether Mr. Richards tried to pressure Frank into selling his place or not?"

"Having you carry Iggy in is better," Rihanna said. "Asking Gavin to spy on his grandfather would be hard for him. I think he said his grandfather was a little hard of hearing, so Iggy will have to speak up."

I smiled. "I'll be sure to tell him. The more I think about this plan, the better it sounds. Basically, Iggy will be invisible the whole time. He can't be harmed."

"True, so who will you use to test Aaron Reed or Ian Silver?" Jaxson asked.

Rihanna grinned. "I was hoping you'd help us out. Drake said you'd spoken to both of them."

"I have. I guess I could pull it off using some ruse for needing to speak with them again."

"I have an idea," I said. "You could always comment to Aaron that I suspect Glen of being a warlock. Does he know anything about that? He'll say no, of course. By that time Iggy will have done his little sting. I can give you say, three minutes, and then call you so you'll have an excuse to leave. What do you think?"

Jaxson smiled. "I like it, but Iggy and I will figure it out ourselves."

"Suit yourself. And for Heath Richards?" I asked. "Who do we use?"

Rihanna looked over at Andorra. "What about your grandmother? She already spoke with him today. She could call him back and ask to clarify something."

Andorra nodded. "I think she'll be willing to do that. Having Iggy there will be good, too. Once he does his howdy-do for Heath, Iggy can chat with Hugo."

"Great," I said. "Who are we missing?"

"We gave Jane Collins a one, since burning the building wouldn't really help Frank," Drake reminded me.

"I agree. How about we start with these people and then regroup?"

I got a thumbs up from everyone. "Great. Maybe tonight Rihanna can talk with Casi and get it set up with her brother. Tomorrow, I'll try to connect with him and Frank, and then Jaxson can head on over to the fire station with Iggy."

"I can do that," Rihanna said.

We all finished our dinner, ready to speak with Terry Alden, Aaron's girlfriend—or rather Glen Harmony's former girlfriend—at the library.

We probably should have asked Andorra's friend, Sylvia, to join us since she was Terry's friend, too, but having five people descend on her could be uncomfortable. In fact, I might have Andorra and my lie detector cousin to speak with Terry while Jaxson, Drake, and myself pretended to be busy doing something else in the library.

After we paid, I asked my aunt if she could keep an eye on Iggy. She said Iggy had gone upstairs to visit with Aimee. That worked for me. We split up into two cars and headed to the library.

"Do you think Iggy will be okay with all of the undercover stuff?" Rihanna asked.

I almost laughed. "Are you kidding? It will be the highlight of his month. Mind you, I'll have to pony up for some great flowers for him to eat. Cloaking himself takes a lot out of him."

"My little buddy will do fine," Jaxson said with pride in his voice.

"He will." I had every faith in my familiar.

Once we arrived at the library, I made my suggestion

about splitting into two groups. "Andorra, you and Rihanna should go first and talk with Terry. Then Jaxson, Drake, and I will go in."

"Works for me." Andorra and Rihanna slipped inside.

My stomach was doing little flips. I hope this wasn't a wild goose chase, but the notion that Glen's former girlfriend had been burned without getting near a flame had a lot of potential.

After giving them a minute, the three of us entered the library. The moment I spotted Dahlia working behind the desk, I relaxed. "I'm going to talk to my friend for a bit," I told Jaxson.

"Go ahead. My brother and I will find something of interest to check out."

I'm sure they would. Dahlia spotted me and smiled.

"Hey, stranger. What's up?" She leaned across the circulation desk and gave me a quick hug.

"Keeping busy. Did you hear about the fire at Candles bookstore?"

"Yes, it's horrible. In the end, it might be for the best, though."

I stiffened. Dahlia was the nicest person I knew. "What do you mean?"

"People aren't reading paper books anymore. I've stopped by their shop a few times, and it's always empty. Whenever I go—which is usually to pick up some non-book item like a candle or some cards—Betty looks so sad. It's depressing seeing what you love slowly die."

Because of the poor economic outlook, their bookstore deserved to burn down? Naturally, I wouldn't voice my opinion. "You believe she's better off not running the store?"

"I don't think she *wants* to run it anymore."

That was the first I'd heard of it. "She told you that?"

"Yes, but Frank loves being there. He'd be lost without having something to do." I'd heard the opposite. Dahlia waved a hand. "Look at this place. It's a library, full of wonderful adventures, and yet not many come here anymore either. In fact, the city just laid off our newest hire because of the lack of traffic."

"That is so sad."

"I know. Joel is convinced that if people want to read a book, they will buy it, not check it out. He's bitter. He loved working here."

My mind tried to connect the dots. It must be because I had arson on my mind that I jumped to a dark place. "You don't think Joel had anything to do with the destruction of the bookstore?"

"No, why would he?"

"Burning the store might lessen the competition with the library." Okay, that was a stretch, but it was all I had.

"That's crazy. Joel loves books. He'd never destroy them."

I wanted to ask if he'd mentioned being a warlock, but most people with powers didn't announce it to just anyone. "Good to know."

My cousin came back. "We're good."

That meant they'd finished grilling Terry. I looked over to where they had been chatting. "Where's Andorra?"

"Looking for the men."

"Good." I turned back to Dahlia. "We will catch up."

"For sure."

We all met back at the car. "Want to regroup at the ice cream shop?" I asked. "Or didn't you learn anything?"

"Terry wasn't all that forthcoming, but Rihanna and I can share our thoughts," Andorra said.

"Great. The ice cream shop it is."

I needed something sweet to get me through the next few days anyway. Talking with Frank was going to be hard. On purpose, I didn't ask Rihanna any questions on the drive back to town since I wanted to hear what Andorra had to say when we were all together.

Even though it was a Friday night, we found a table large enough for all of us. After we ordered, we returned to our seats. "Tell me. I'm excited to hear what Terry said."

Andorra inhaled. "We first chatted about why she and Glen broke up, which is pertinent to the case."

"I'm listening."

"Glen became increasingly angry over the last few months. It was due in part to the fact that his father started drinking again."

"That would upset anyone," Jaxson said.

"Yes, but it is why he started drinking that is interesting."

I had no idea where she was going with this. "Do tell."

"Mr. Harmony worked in Summertime, managing a dry cleaning store. Can you guess who owned the building?"

The pieces fell. "Heath Richards."

"Yup."

"Next, you're going to tell me that Mr. Harmony's building was the one Richards shut down."

"Bingo."

I blew out a breath. I dove into my mint chocolate chip

ice cream to wrap my thoughts around things. "Do you think Glen, or his little brother, decided to get back at Mr. Richards by setting the building on fire? If so, that would mean it had nothing to do with Frank and Betty Sanchez."

"Could be, but here is the most interesting part."

"I thought the first tidbit was good," I said.

"Maybe. Remember, Silvia mentioned that Terry had been burned but didn't know how?"

"Sure." It was why we'd spoken with her in the first place. "What did she say about it?"

"Rihanna can confirm that Terry was telling the truth when she said that Aaron had stopped over at the library to see her. In the middle of their conversation, Glen stopped by to pick her up. When he saw them together, he got mad and grabbed her arm. To the outsider, it might not seem like much, but she felt the heat."

The word heat set my neurons firing. "Heat, as in a potential fire source?"

"She didn't catch on fire, but his hand was super hot. She didn't say anything at the moment, because Aaron was there, and she liked him."

I could fill in the blanks. "But the next day, she noticed blisters—not bruises—where Glen had grabbed her."

"Exactly."

"She wasn't totally forthcoming," Rihanna said.

We all stopped. "Are you saying she wasn't burned?" I asked.

"No, that part is true, but I know she's hiding something."

"Any idea what that would be?"

She pressed her lips together. "I just heard words like soda and flames."

That was cryptic. "Did you ask her about it?"

Rihanna shook her head. "She was too scared. I had the sense telling us about the burn was already out of her comfort zone."

I looked over at Jaxson. "Maybe when you have your chat with Aaron, you can ask him about it. I bet Terry gave him more details."

"I can give it a try."

"Should we raise Glen's number higher?" I asked.

"Absolutely. I thought Heath Richards had been guilty, but I'm going to change my mind and pick Glen," Andorra said.

"What happens if we find out Glen's not a warlock?" I asked.

No surprise, everyone was silent. "How about we wait until that happens?" Jaxson said. He is always level-headed.

"I'm good with that. Tomorrow, we'll start Operation Warlock Detection."

That brought smiles to everyone. We finished our dessert and headed out.

"Text us what happens with Frank after you speak with him," Andorra said.

"Can do."

Chapter Ten

"**A**RE YOU READY?" I asked Iggy the next morning.

He lifted his head. "I was born ready."

I was right in assuming Iggy would be excited to take part in this discovery operation. "I don't know how long my discussion with Frank and Betty Sanchez will take. I need to pick his brain for a bit, so we might be there a while. On the other hand, it's also possible the fire wasn't about him, so Frank might not know much. The arson might be about getting revenge against Mr. Richards for shutting down the strip mall, which means we could be in and out."

"Either way, I know what to do. I'll cloak myself and then get real close to Mr. Sanchez. I'll be sure to yell in his ear."

I laughed. "You don't have to go that far. Most likely Betty will be sitting next to him."

"Great. Then I can call out both of their names."

That was a good idea. "You do that."

I already had called Frank, and he almost sounded excited to talk to someone about the fire. If he'd been guilty, he would have said he wasn't up to chatting. I had planned to visit him later in the week but figuring out who was a warlock couldn't wait.

Once Iggy hopped in my purse, we took off. "When will I

know to start the undercover operation?" he asked as I placed him on the car seat.

"As soon as I put my bag down, you should cloak yourself, crawl out, and do your thing."

"I won't let you down."

I adored Iggy. "You never do."

Once I found Frank and Betty's home, I parked on the street and went up to the front door. Just as I was about to knock, Frank opened up, taking me by surprise. "Hi, Glinda."

I was a little uncertain of the protocol. He had lost his business, but he sounded surprisingly upbeat. Did that mean I shouldn't hug him? When he stepped inside, I followed his lead and entered. No hug. Betty was standing by the sofa.

"Hi, Betty." I was about to motion she sit down, when she asked if I wanted to have a drink. I didn't, but she seemed like she needed to do something. "Tea would be fine."

Frank sat on the sofa, and I took the chair across from him. I placed my purse on the floor out of view from the couch in case Iggy's cloaking failed.

"I am so sorry about the store. I never imagined something like this would ever happen."

"Me neither, but truth be told, after Daniel left us some money, we decided it was time to retire."

"That's great." At least I think it was. "If that is what you want, that is?"

Betty returned, handed me a tea, and she then explained about her arthritis. "As much as I hate to give up running the bookstore, it's time."

"Did Heath Richards suggest you sell your store by any chance?"

Frank chuckled. "Indirectly, yes. Mr. Richards explained that he was losing money mostly because of the low rent that several of us pay. I understood. His dad was a poor business-man. He told us that either we paid more for rent, or he might be forced to close down the whole strip of businesses, which would do irrefutable damage to not only the owners but to Witch's Cove itself."

"That would be terrible. Actually, more than terrible. People might be forced to move elsewhere."

"I agree."

"Hey, Frank!" Iggy shouted.

I actually jerked at the sound of my familiar's voice, even though I was expecting him to call out. Darn. Either Frank was really hard of hearing, or he wasn't a warlock, which was what I suspected.

"Betty, can you hear me?" Iggy asked. He got the same response—which was no response.

While I couldn't see my familiar, he probably crawled down the sofa, padded across the carpet, and slipped back into my purse.

"Do either of you have any idea who might have set the fire?"

Both shook their heads. "The only one who deserved to be angry with me is no longer with us," Frank said.

I figured he was talking about Ian Silver's dad. "You received no threats of any kind, didn't owe anyone money, or anything like that?"

Frank looked over at his wife. She shrugged. "No. What happened is terrible. We're just happy the fire didn't spread. We're going to try to move on. Once Gavin goes to college, we might even move to Arizona. My arthritis might be better out there."

"I understand, but Witch's Cove would miss you both." I figured by now Iggy was probably chomping at the bit to get out of there. Patience wasn't his forte. I stood. "If you think of anything that might help us find out who did this, be sure to let Steve know."

"We will."

"Thanks for talking to me. Once more, I'm sorry for your loss."

I really did sound like the daughter of a funeral home director. As soon as I left, I climbed into my car and started the engine. I looked over at Iggy. "Good job."

"Thank you, but they weren't special."

"No, not special like you. I'm pretty sure you'll find a warlock or two before we're done, though."

"I hope so. Who's next?"

"I'll see if Christian is up for taking you for a spin."

"A spin? That's cute, but I'm up for it. I know what to do now."

I thought he knew what to do before. As we neared the garage where Christian worked, I pulled over to give Casi's brother a call. Rihanna had spoken with her good friend who'd promised to explain to Christian what he needed to do. Apparently, he was excited to see Iggy work his magic. Even though Christian was a warlock, he didn't know if Glen was one or not. His coworker never said anything or showed any signs, but Christian wasn't going to rule it out.

He answered on the first ring. "Hey, Christian. Are you ready to have Iggy do his thing with Glen, assuming he's there?"

"Sure, but why not come in. We can talk about some imaginary car problem you're having. In the meantime, Iggy can test Glen."

I hadn't thought of that, but I was game. "Good idea."

I drove to the garage and parked. I patted my purse to let him know to be ready. Since Iggy heard our conversation, he'd know what to do. I stepped inside the garage and set my purse down at my feet.

"What's the problem with the car?" Christian asked, loud enough for Glen to hear.

I had to make up something or Glen might become suspicious. "It knocks and stalls at the most inopportune times." That wasn't far off. Someday, I'd have to get a new car.

"What kind of gas do you use?" he asked.

I looked to see where Glen had gone, but he'd disappeared. I faced Christian. "Where's Glen?" I whispered.

He looked behind him. "In the bay in back."

"I hope Iggy is safe back there." No telling how dangerous it could be.

"He should be fine. How big is he again?"

I'd forgotten that Christian had yet to meet my infamous familiar. "About nine pounds and so long, excluding the tail." I used my hands to indicate his length.

"I'll check on him if he doesn't come back in a minute."

Something scratched my leg. "Never mind. He's here." I felt my purse sag from Iggy's added weight. I lifted it up and held open my purse for Christian to see. "This is Iggy."

"I thought your familiar was male. She's pink!"

Not good. I'd never hear the end of it now. "Iggy is a boy.

Long story—one I don't have time to tell." I turned to my familiar. "So, did you-know-who respond?"

"Nope, and I called his name a few times."

"And you were invisible the whole time?"

"Yup."

Darn. I was really hoping Glen was our warlock. I turned back to Christian. "Thanks again for helping."

"Sorry, you didn't find your man—or rather your warlock."

"Yeah. Me, too."

I left and then sat in the car for a minute before leaving, a bit upset at what happened—or rather what didn't happen. I really thought Rihanna's plan had been a solid one, but we were quickly running out of suspects.

"Do I really look like a girl?" Iggy asked.

"No. Not at all. Christian didn't know that only males have a crest on top of their head and bodies."

"Yeah. Dumb Christian."

I was glad Iggy didn't throw a tantrum. I inhaled. Jaxson was up next. He would use Iggy to test Ian Silver and Aaron Reed, but I highly doubted Ian was a warlock, though it was possible Aaron was.

Once back at the office, I put my purse on the sofa and let Iggy get out and stretch.

"How did it go?" Jaxson asked.

"No warlocks."

Jaxson's brows rose. "Nothing from Glen?" I shook my head. "That surprises me."

"Iggy, are you sure Glen heard you? He could have been wearing headphones or earbuds," I said.

"Now you're being insulting. Trust me. I tried a few times to get his attention. I even crawled in front of him and called his name. Nothing."

Iggy had a rather distinctive voice—almost squeaky one might say. I turned to Jaxson. "Do you think Christian tipped him off?"

"Why would he? If anything, Christian would want Glen to look suspicious. We are pretty certain someone with magic set the fire. If we can't find any witches or warlocks, Christian might think we'd pin it on him—which we wouldn't do—but people who grow up getting into trouble are used to being accused of things they weren't involved in."

He had a point. "I don't know what to think. Let's see what happens with our firemen."

"I need food," Iggy said.

I understood how much it took to cloak oneself. "I have just the thing." I went into the kitchen and grabbed the flowers from the refrigerator that I'd purchased earlier. "Here ya go."

Iggy munched them down. "These are great," he mumbled in between bites.

"How does this work?" Jaxson asked. "I'm not carrying a purse into the station."

I laughed. "I have a day pack. I'll leave the zipper undone, and Iggy will take care of the rest."

"Sounds good."

"Do you know if either man is at work? Ian Silver could be at the bookstore checking out the fire."

"I'll take my chances. If neither are there, I'll find out when they plan to return and go back then."

"You are the best."

As soon as Iggy finished his meal, Jaxson gathered him up. I hoped that cloaking and recloaking so many times in a day didn't harm him in any way like it had me when I'd done it.

"What do you plan to do while I'm gone?" Jaxson asked.

"The last step in our plan is to see if Heath Richards is a warlock. I need to talk to Bertha about setting up a meeting with him."

"Smart." Jaxson leaned over and gave me a goodbye kiss. "Wish us luck."

"Luck."

I pulled out the whiteboard and noted which suspects had failed the warlock test. The only surprise had been Glen. I'd been so sure he was guilty.

After I studied the facts again, I was no closer to figuring out who'd set the fire than before I did the test. It was time to head on over to the Hex and Bones in order to brainstorm a feasible way for Heath Richards to return to the store without becoming suspicious that we were up to something.

I grabbed my phone and keys and headed out. When I entered the store, I was pleased to see both Andorra and Bertha there. I guess Elizabeth had the day off—or else she was working a later shift.

Andorra came over. "Hey, how did it go with our *suspects?*"

I really liked this woman. Drake had picked well. "It was a no-go on Frank, Betty, and Glen."

She hissed in a breath. "That's disappointing."

"I know. Iggy is with Jaxson now. I'm hoping he'll have more success with Ian and Aaron."

"Let's hope. What's the plan with Heath and Iggy?"

"That's what I'd like to discuss with Bertha."

Andorra smiled. "I'll let her know you need to chat."

Andorra manned the store while Bertha and I went into the back. While I didn't mind Hugo being there, having him in his human form meant a threat still existed.

Bertha led us over to the chairs that she hadn't moved since the last time we were there. "I have an idea," she said.

I was glad one of us did. "Tell me."

Chapter Eleven

"HEATH RICHARDS ASKED me to consider letting him increase my rent. Just so you know, I'm fine with it. I told him I'd think about it and get back with him. I realize I could call him and tell him that, but I understand we need him here," Bertha said.

"We do. There needs to be something else you can lure him here with besides agreeing to his new rent terns."

Bertha smiled. "How about if we kill two birds with one stone?"

I had no idea what she was talking about. "Meaning what?"

"I thought we could do something to help out Mr. Richards as well as help the community. I could ask him to stop over so we could discuss this new plan of mine."

"What exactly are you wanting to do?" She was being rather secretive, even for her.

"How about if we tell him we are planning to have a fundraiser to help with the repairs for his building? If this strip of stores is in danger of closing, as he claims, the whole town will suffer."

"It will. Frank told me the same thing, so yeah, your idea sounds great. I'm sure the good citizens of Witch's Cove would be willing to pony up a few bucks to save their town."

"I'm so glad you're on board! I know you want to find out who burned down the bookstore, and I want that too, but making sure Heath Richards doesn't close us first is important."

"I totally agree. I'll help anyway I can. I'm sure Aunt Fern, Dolly, Maude, Miriam, and Pearl will do what they can, too. They love to organize things."

"Thank you. How about I call Mr. Richards and see when he can come over?" Bertha asked.

"Sure, but we need Iggy here, and at the moment he's with Jaxson to see if either Aaron Reed or Ian Silver have magic."

"No problem. Once Iggy is free, call me."

I hugged her. "Will do."

With that chore complete, I returned to the office to await the results of Jaxson's investigation. After all of the jobs we'd worked on, I shouldn't be nervous, but I was, though I couldn't figure out why. Perhaps it was the thought of something tearing apart this town that petrified me.

I inhaled deeply and gave myself a bit of a pep talk. "Fundraiser, Glinda. Work on Bertha's fundraiser idea." I'd actually thought of a few things on the walk back from Hex and Bones and was ready to get started.

I was lucky. The queen of big events was my Aunt Fern. After the potential arsonist was caught, I planned to put all of my energy into making this the best fundraiser this town had ever seen.

First though, Jaxson had to return with Iggy. Once he did, I'd call Bertha to say we were ready. In turn, she would speak with Mr. Richards and let us know when to stop over.

In the meantime, I needed to think about how to raise money—a lot of it. Being spring, the weather would be perfect for a large outdoor event. I wasn't sure who to contact about renting some circus rides, like a Ferris wheel and such, but we'd had them in Witch's Cove in the past. The mayor must have some contacts that he could call.

I grabbed a piece of paper and broke it into six parts—one for each aspect of this big event. I'd ask each of the women to organize one thing. Since Pearl was rather old, she might be in charge of hiring the security, but I'd let them decide who wanted to do what.

Just as I was about finished with a very rough draft of how the town could raise money, Jaxson and Iggy returned.

I spun around. "So?"

He set down the backpack, and Iggy raced out. "I was so good," my familiar announced.

"Why is that?"

Jaxson cocked a brow. "Tell her, Iggy. It was your show."

Iggy pranced up to me. "First, we spoke with Aaron. I liked him."

"I didn't think your job was to make friends."

"I know. Don't worry. I cloaked myself and snuck up behind him, not that he could see me. Then I shouted: Boo! Aaron jumped so high I cracked myself up. I always thought firefighters had nerves of steel."

I turned to Jaxson. "Is that what you witnessed?"

"Yes, ma'am. Aaron spun around but couldn't see Iggy. Neither could I, of course. He then asked if I'd said something, to which I responded with a resounding no."

"I'm not sure I could have kept a straight face," I said.

"It was hard. Operation Warlock Detection was a success."

"What about Ian?" I kind of liked Aaron, too. Secretly, I was hoping he hadn't been one.

"Nope, not even a hair raised. Iggy ran around the man, yelling at him, but there was no response."

"I can't believe that Aaron might be our arsonist, though it is possible that Heath Richards could be one since we haven't tested him yet."

Jaxson sat down on the sofa and patted the seat. I slipped next to him.

"The facts might point to Aaron, but something is off. He acted very concerned about the fire, fearing this person would try again."

"Maybe he was playing you."

Jaxson shook his head. "I'm not saying he couldn't have, but I'm pretty good at spotting a liar."

"That's fair."

"Speaking of our other possible suspect, how did it go with Bertha?" he asked.

I detailed how she was going to get Heath to show up. "The good part is that we really are going to try to raise money to save the building."

His brows rose. "That's fantastic. Even if we never figure out who torched the bookstore, maybe we can keep Heath from having to close the stores."

"Exactly."

"Do you know yet what you are going to do in order to accomplish this large fundraising task?" he asked.

I rolled my eyes. "I've only been back a few minutes. Okay, I kind of have a plan."

I showed him my list of who might be willing to help and what areas needed to be covered.

He whistled. "That is impressive."

"I'm not sure how long it will take for Heath to get back to Bertha, but maybe I can set up a meeting with the six women to get their input."

Jaxson nodded. "You could hold the meeting in that back room of Hex and Bones. If you take Iggy with you, and if Heath shows up, you can see if he is a warlock."

I smiled. "You are a smart man. I'll call the ladies now and see when we can meet—right after I contact Bertha to see if we can use her place."

"I get to see Hugo again?" Iggy asked.

"Yes, assuming he is still human, which I bet he is." He'd been in his human form only a few minutes ago. I don't know why he'd change back now.

"Yay!"

We didn't have any time to waste, so I called Bertha and told her about my plan, including the fact that Iggy and I were ready.

"I'll contact him right now. As for you using the back room as a meeting place, of course you can. I think this is exciting. Let me know if you want me to call any of the women."

That would save time. "Sure. How about I take Aunt Fern, Dolly, and Gertrude, and you call the rest? If they can't meet now, ask them to give you their available times, and I'll coordinate a date."

"That sounds awesome. I'll get right on it," she said.

"Super." I hung up, feeling quite satisfied. I turned to Jaxson and told him what Bertha said. "We'll need to tell Steve and then the mayor about this new scheme. I want to be sure we can do this."

He chuckled. "Go ahead, but I imagine both will be happy to help. However, be aware that this fundraiser might cause the arsonist to strike again." He held up a hand. "I'm not saying that's a bad thing since this time we'll be ready for him."

"Why would supporting the town cause the arsonist to strike again?" I don't know why things weren't making sense to me all of sudden.

"I'd be guessing, but if the fire is about getting back at Heath Richards by destroying his building, if you hold a fundraiser to prop him up, wouldn't that upset the arsonist even more? If he's smart, he'll want to do further damage after the repairs are complete. That means he might wait weeks or months before striking again. Being on high alert for that long would require a lot of energy."

"You have a point. Rihanna mentioned something about Wilt Harmony saying that Mr. Richards deserved to pay, but Glen is not a warlock so he can't be the arsonist. Then who is?"

"I don't know, but how do you explain Glen being able to touch his former girlfriend and burn her if he doesn't have magic?" he asked.

"I can't."

"Maybe you should ask Gertrude. I have the power to talk with Iggy and yet I'm not a warlock. My ability is the result of a spell. Maybe Glen's is too."

"Wow. I hadn't thought of that. Are you thinking someone might have put a spell on Glen that made his hands turn into blow torches?"

Jaxson shrugged. "What do I know? I'm simply a human."

He knew a lot. "I'll call Bertha to let her know I might be delayed. If she calls and says Heath is ready to come over, can you take Iggy over to the shop and have him yell at Mr. Richards?"

He chuckled. "Absolutely."

I made my two calls. The first was to Bertha to tell her about Glen's possible situation. "Have you ever heard of such a spell?"

"I honestly can't say I have, though I know humans can be given magical powers for a short time. If Glen is guilty, I'm not so sure he could burn Terry and still set a store on fire a few weeks later. That seems like a pretty powerful spell—if it exists. I suggest you speak with Levy or his grandmother."

"Thanks. I will. I need to talk with Gertrude about our fundraiser anyway."

"I'll see what I can uncover."

"That would be great. The more eyes on this, the better." I remembered Jaxson's warning. "As for the fundraiser, how about holding off on contacting the ladies, if you haven't called them yet."

"I haven't, but why?"

I told her it might cause the arsonist to delay striking again until after the repairs are done. "I'm not good at waiting, but I have a plan, sort of, to lure him into striking sooner rather than later. I just need time to flesh it out."

"Sure. Mums the word on the fundraiser. Just tell me when to call."

"Will do." I mentally blew out a breath. Crisis averted—for now. Next, I called the Psychics Corner to see if I could stop in and chat with Gertrude for a few minutes. I got lucky as she would be free shortly.

"I'll be back in a bit," I told Jaxson.

Iggy waddled out. "Can I come? I'd like to say hi to Gertrude."

Those two got along really well. "I know, but what if you're needed for Operation Warlock Detection? That is of utmost importance right now."

"Fine." He spun around and slid under the sofa. What was up with him? He'd been so excited to do the sting operation before. "If you come with me now, you might miss seeing Hugo, and we have no idea how long he'll be in his human form."

Iggy lifted his head. "Okay."

With that settled, I hugged Jaxson goodbye and took off for the Psychics Corner. By the time I reached the building, Gertrude was free to see me. When I entered her office, she motioned I take a seat on the sofa. There on the coffee table sat my glass of sweet iced tea. She knew what I liked. "Thank you."

"You're welcome. What's this about someone being able to set a building on fire with his bare hands?"

"It's a theory." I went through everything I knew, including Glen's failed warlock test. "Could there be a spell to do that?"

Gertrude stood and made her way over to a bookshelf. "The spell might be more of a curse."

A curse, a spell. Same difference to me. "But is it possible?"

"Anything is possible, my dear." She located a book from her bookcase and carried it back. Once she placed it on the coffee table, she thumbed through it. "Here is something that is kind of like what you are describing."

I read the passage. "I admit it has similarities to what might have occurred. The part that really intrigues me is that this spell is used to curb anger, and yet the one time Glen's girlfriend claimed his hands turned hot, he was rather upset."

"Spells don't always go as planned."

She got that right. Look at Iggy. He was supposed to be a cat, and he certainly wasn't supposed to turn out pink. That being said, I wouldn't trade him for the world.

"Is there anything we can do to break this spell—assuming that is what this is?"

"Not that I know of, but you know my grandson. He and his coven often can find that needle in a haystack."

"So true. I'll give him a call."

"Good luck."

My cell beeped, and I looked at the caller ID. "It's Jaxson. It might be about Heath Richards."

"Ah, yes, the one who wants to possibly shut down all those stores."

"Yes. Give me a sec." I glanced at the text. It said Mr. Richards would be at Hex and Bones in fifteen minutes, and that Jaxson would meet me there with Iggy. "I need to go, but I want to discuss a possible fundraiser to help save the town.

No money required, just some mental help."

Gertrude smiled. "I'd be happy to do what I can."

"Thank you. We'll be in touch." I quickly hugged her goodbye and rushed out since I didn't want to miss the meeting with Mr. Richards. I should have asked her to keep quiet about the fundraiser, but I trusted her. She wasn't a gossip.

My plan was to show Mr. Richards my list of assignments and ideas while Iggy snuck up behind him to see if he was a warlock or not. In all honesty, I just couldn't see the owner burning his own building. I hadn't heard of any fires in any of the other towns, so that didn't seem to be his way of doing things.

I crossed the street and dashed into the store. Jaxson was there talking with Andorra. I didn't see Iggy, but I had to assume he was chatting with Hugo—or whatever they did to communicate.

I went up to them. "Anything new?"

"No. We were discussing your fundraiser idea on how to keep Mr. Richards from having to close the stores," Jaxson said.

"It was Bertha's plan."

"But you'll see it become a reality," he said.

"I hope."

"You got this."

Chapter Twelve

M Y JOB AT the moment was two-fold. One was to keep Mr. Heath Richards busy while Iggy determined if he was a warlock and, second, to find out how much we had to raise in order to save the building from shutting down.

"How about checking on Iggy while I chat with Bertha? I want our stories to match," I said to Jaxson.

Jaxson kissed my forehead. "Can do, and don't worry. You'll do great."

Why did he keep saying that? Was it more to convince himself or me? It didn't really matter. I had a job to do. As soon as Jaxson ducked into the back room, I waited for Bertha to finish up with a customer. I then went over to her.

"Hey. Before the owner shows up, let me show you what I've been working on regarding your plan."

"Show me."

I handed her my paper. "I've spoken with Gertrude, and she's on board. When the time is right, I'm hoping you can give some information to the ladies when you talk with them."

"I can do that."

I didn't want to discuss what Gertrude told me in the main room for fear someone might overhear. Just as I was about to suggest we step into the back room for privacy, the front door opened, and Heath Richards walked in. I motioned with my eyes for Andorra to tell Iggy his time had come. Once my familiar was aware of who'd arrived, he would cloak himself and then do his magic.

Mr. Richards waved and made a beeline toward us. Despite it being very warm out, he was sporting a suit that he looked quite handsome in. From the way his jaw was clenched, though, and how dark the circles were under his eyes, the man was at his breaking point.

Bertha introduced us and explained why I was there.

"A fundraiser for these buildings?" he asked.

The joy alone in his eyes convinced me he had nothing to do with burning his own building. "Yes. I thought we could have it in the park with some rides for the kids. I know Tampa has their fairgrounds, and with some pressure from our mayor, maybe we can rent some of their rides for a weekend." I rushed on. "We could have booths that sell cotton candy, fudge, strawberries, and whatever else is in season. There will be something for everyone." I smiled, trying to convince him this was a good idea. "I'm sure I can get some palm readers and fortune tellers, too."

He sputtered, seemingly in shock. "That sounds fantastic. I can't thank you enough. When would this incredible event take place?"

I didn't want to commit before I'd spoken with everyone. "I don't have a date yet since I wanted to see if you were okay with it."

"Of course, I'm okay with it. Heck, I'm more than okay. This is sensational." He sobered a bit. "What do you see the money being used for exactly?"

I nodded at Bertha to answer since she was a store owner.

"The roof leaks in a few places, and the wiring definitely needs to be updated," she said.

"Consider it done when the funds are in place."

"Do you think you could figure out how much money you'd need so you won't have to shut down the stores?" I asked.

While I didn't see my familiar since he'd cloaked himself, Jaxson was standing at the entrance implying Iggy was somewhere.

"Oh, Heath Richards!" Iggy shouted.

I swear every witch or warlock in the store would have heard him, which could prove troublesome.

"I'd be happy to. I'll only need a day or two to come up with the numbers." Mr. Richards didn't flinch at the sound of Iggy's voice. While he might be faking it, I doubted it.

That meant Aaron and possibly Glen had magic. I hoped we weren't being short-sighted by ignoring someone else. While I had Mr. Richard's attention, it wouldn't hurt to ask him about the fire. I started by letting him know that I was an amateur sleuth who wanted to help Frank Sanchez find out who'd set his bookstore on fire.

"That's outstanding. I want to know, too. Naturally." Heath Richards sounded sincere.

"Do you know who might have it in for you?"

"Got a piece of paper and a pen?" His brows rose, but I couldn't tell if he was kidding or not. "I'm serious," he said when neither of us moved.

"I'll get something to write on," Bertha said.

"There are that many people you've upset?" I asked.

"Sad to say, yes. I recently had to do one of the hardest things I've ever had to do in my life—close a lot of businesses. Basically, I ruined many people's lives. If I knew that would happen, why did I do it? Simple, I've run out of money. The low rent doesn't cover the cost of running the building, not to mention the increase in taxes. Twenty years ago, these buildings didn't need nearly the upkeep they do today."

"That makes sense."

Bertha returned with the paper. "Here you go."

"I'll list the names of the owners. Could one of them want revenge enough to do this? Sure. Could I guess which one? No."

While not great, it was a start. He neatly printed the names. "Why target Witch's Cove instead of where you'd closed the building?"

"Excellent question. I wish I had the answer for you."

He kept writing. It was when I spotted the last name of Harmony that my pulse shot up. "Did Mr. Harmony manage a dry cleaning store by any chance?"

I wanted to be positive it wasn't Wilt and Glen's uncle or some other Harmony.

"He did."

"How angry was he when he lost his job?"

Heath Richards studied me. "What's this about?"

As much as I wanted to tell him about the Harmony sons, without proof I didn't want to malign either of them—or tip anyone off. "Just curious."

"I heard he took it hard. Most of the people who run a small business are not wealthy, and Al had never been one to save much. I tried talking to each owner after the closing, but he wouldn't take my calls."

That told me a lot. "Thanks for your help. If you could draft a proposal for what you need and email it to me, that would be great." I tore off a piece of paper and wrote down my contact information.

"Will do." He looked over at Bertha. "We'll be in touch."

"Sure."

As soon as he left, Jaxson and Andorra came over. "What did he say?"

I gave them the lowdown. "Considering he's not a warlock, together with his excitement about the fundraiser, and coupled with his willingness to give us the names of those other business owners, I'd say he's innocent."

"You are probably right," Jaxson shot back, "but remember that Glen didn't test positive for being a warlock either."

"True, but we know that Glen's hands can heat up. Yes, I know, Heath Richards might be part dragon with the ability to shoot fire out of his fingertips, but I don't think so. He looked genuinely distraught."

"A dragon?" Jaxson worked hard not to laugh.

"Yes. I wouldn't have believed it either, but then I met Hugo. Before, I had only believed shapeshifters came in the form of werewolves, but who's to say that dragons don't exist?"

"Sure, pink lady." Jaxson turned to Bertha. "What do you think about Mr. Richards?"

"I agree with Glinda," Bertha said. "I've dealt with magic my whole life, and this guy doesn't have any abilities, nor is he capable of harming anyone."

"Okay, that leaves us with Glen and Aaron," he said.

I told them about my discussion with Gertrude.

"She actually thinks that Glen might have been cursed?" Jaxson asked.

I shrugged. "She said it's possible. Personally, I'm open to anything at this point. And by open, I mean I'll give Levy a call to see if his coven can help learn more about that kind of spell."

Andorra's eyes lit up. "Do you think you could take me to see this library? Memaw hasn't stopped talking about how amazing it is."

I smiled, pulled out my phone, and waved it. "I will certainly ask."

I stepped into the back room for some privacy. I didn't spot Iggy and had to assume he was wandering somewhere in the store. I called my warlock friend, who by now must be getting tired of all of my requests.

"Hey, Glinda. We're still looking for a warlock who can set things on fire. Sorry it's taking so long."

"That's okay. Actually, a warlock might not be involved after all." I explained about the results of Operation Warlock Detection. "The thing is, the one who didn't turn out to be a warlock can heat his hands when he is angry. Your grandmother thought Glen might have been cursed—or been given a spell to reduce his anger—not actually been the one to perform the spell. Clearly, the anger reduction part didn't work."

Levy whistled. "We can turn our attention to curses rather than talents of a warlock. I imagine the two are connected."

"That would be great. I really do think we've narrowed it down to two men, but we can't do much until they try something again." Only then did it occur to me that we had no plan if we caught this arsonist. "While you are looking into this—assuming you are willing to do so—can you see if there is an antidote to this curse?"

"We'll look, but I'm not that hopeful. Antidotes are not always listed in a spell book for obvious reasons."

"That's disappointing but understandable." I waited for him to suggest I stop over at the library, but he might know his people were busy. "I appreciate it."

"We'll work as fast as we can."

Just as I hung up, Iggy crawled into the back room. "Whatcha doing back here?" he asked.

I picked him up and placed him on a shelf near Hugo. "Speaking with Levy."

"About what?"

Wasn't he the curious one? Sometimes I found that if I talked things out, the answer often came to me. "We think we've narrowed it down to two arsonists: Aaron and Glen."

"Glen isn't a warlock."

I expected that comeback. "I know, but if his hands heat up when he is angry, Gertrude thinks someone might have put a curse on him—or a spell to help decrease his anger."

"That was an epic fail," Iggy said.

I chuckled. "Spells aren't foolproof."

"Don't I know it. So now what?"

"I asked Levy if he and his coven could find the antidote."

Iggy looked over at Hugo. My familiar stared at him for at least thirty seconds. I had to assume they were communicating. Iggy turned back to me. "If Glen can set things on fire when his hands are hot, why don't you cool them off?"

I laughed at the simplicity until I gave it a few seconds consideration. "How do we do that? It's not like we can ask him to dip his hands in a bucket of ice water."

Iggy conferred with Hugo again. "Hugo said that he can wrap the cursed man's hands in ice."

I looked over at Andorra's mute familiar. "How?"

Iggy waited patiently, nodding occasionally. "He's a little insulted you would question him, but he forgives you. Hugo has extensive powers, or did you forget?

He had been able to get someone to spill the beans on our last case. "I didn't forget. What can he do exactly?"

"While he can't shoot fire out of his mouth, like many gargoyles can, he can freeze things using magic, not actual water," Iggy announced.

Gargoyles could shoot fire out of their mouths? Were they descendants of dragons? Oh, I had so much to learn. "What happens when this magic ice thaws, assuming it does?" I didn't understand how this all worked, though of late, that seemed to be an all-too common occurrence.

"The curse will be broken."

What? "Let me get this straight. If—and that is a big if— Glen Harmony comes in here ready to burn the place down, Hugo would sneak out of the back room and somehow freeze Glen's hands?"

"Yes," Iggy said, answering for Hugo.

"Has he ever done something like this before?" I asked my familiar.

Iggy listened and then translated. "No, but it shouldn't be a problem."

"What's to prevent Glen from taking one look at Hugo

and running away?" I didn't add that would be likely since Hugo was not only a bit stiff but rather scary looking.

"He won't give Glen the chance."

A second after Iggy told me that, Hugo teleported next to me and exerted a slight pressure on my shoulder. While it didn't hurt, the result was that I couldn't move. "Hugo? What did you do to me?"

He touched me again, and I was back to my usual self. I let out a long breath. "I see. You have many talents. Good to know that you can sneak up on someone, paralyze them for a moment, encase their hands in some kind of magical ice, before retiring to your back room. In the end, Glen, or whoever is guilty, will be unable to set anything on fire again, right?"

A few seconds later, Iggy answered. "That's right."

My mind was blown. Jaxson came into the back room. "Is there a party I'm missing?"

"You have no idea what Iggy just told me."

Chapter Thirteen

"TELL ME," JAXSON said.

"You won't believe what Hugo can do." I listed his amazing talents. "If this works, all we need is to lure the arsonist here and then let Hugo take over."

Jaxson's brows pinched. "Are you planning on putting up a sign that says: burn this store down?"

I punched him lightly in the arm. "Funny. I haven't had time to think it through."

Jaxson picked up Iggy. "I think we should let Steve know what we've found out. He needs to be aware who is and who isn't a warlock and how we plan to stop this person."

"Perfect. I also want to tell him about the fundraiser, but first I want to talk to Andorra about something and tell Levy he can halt his search for an antidote to Glen's curse. How about I meet you back at the office?"

Logistically that made no sense since the sheriff's office was only a half a block away on the same side of the street, but I wanted to speak with her alone. I dipped my eyes at Iggy, hoping Jaxson would understand.

"No problem. See you back there."

As soon as he and Iggy headed out, I called Levy and explained about the talented gargoyle.

"That's fantastic. I'd love to meet him."

"I'd love for that to happen, but Hugo is usually in his stone form. And he only communicates with his host and Iggy."

"I might have to stop over when she's there."

"Please do, but don't take too long."

We chatted a bit more and then I went out to my friend. I wanted to make sure what Hugo said was possible. I had no proof that Iggy hadn't made it all up, though my familiar wasn't prone to lying.

"Hey, can we talk for a bit?" I asked.

"Sure."

"Let's go in the back. It involves your *friend*."

She smiled. "Gotcha."

Once back there, I turned to Hugo. "Please don't take offense, but Iggy can exaggerate."

"He didn't," Andorra said after listening to something Hugo told her. "What's this about?" she asked me.

I gave her the full rundown of what I learned from Gertrude's curse theory to Hugo's offer to freeze the arsonist's hands. "You can see why I wanted the confirmation."

"For sure and wow." She turned to Hugo. "Can you really do that?" She nodded a few times, acting much like Iggy had. "Seems as if Iggy's interpretation was spot on."

"Okay. I'm going to speak with Steve about beefing up security around here, but I want to get Aaron's take on just how hot Glen's hands had been when he grabbed Terry."

"You think she exaggerated?"

I shrugged. "She might have been so bitter against her former boyfriend that she exaggerated a bit."

"You're smart to find out more. Memaw told me about her fundraiser idea. Count me in."

I smiled. "You are the best." I then had to break it to her about how I didn't get invited to meet with the coven at the library."

"That's okay. Maybe another time."

"For sure."

"And don't worry about finding enough people to help with the fundraiser. I'll rope Drake into having a wine tasting booth or something. It will help the town as well as his business."

"Smart." I didn't want to keep Iggy and Jaxson waiting. "We'll be in touch. I'll email you my plan for the fundraiser, but we'll need to hold off telling everyone for a bit." I wasn't sure if her grandmother had filled her in.

"Why?"

Apparently, she hadn't. "We need to catch this arsonist first before we do the fundraiser and spiff up the building."

"I don't understand."

"I'm going out on a limb here by saying Glen is our guy."

"Okay."

"Let's suppose the arsonist wants to retaliate against Heath Richards for shutting down the mall in Summertime."

Andorra nodded. "I'm following so far."

"If we announce this fundraiser, who knows when he'll strike next."

Andorra's eyes widened. "You think he'd wait until after the repairs are done before burning down another store?"

"Exactly. That way, he'd do the most damage. All this means is that we need to spread the rumor that if Mr.

Richards suffers even one more blow—or rather has another fire—he will have to shut this place down."

"You're baiting him?" she asked.

Baiting was a harsh word. "I guess, but I want us to be ready for him before we put the word out."

"How? Witch's Cove has all of two law enforcement agents."

That was a problem. "Steve could ask Misty to lend him some of her officers from Liberty."

She grimaced. "For a night maybe, but this guy—Glen—might wait weeks."

"What do you suggest?"

"I need to think about it, but how about if we gather our gossip queens and see what they can come up with."

"Tell them the truth and the whole truth? Including that we suspect Glen?"

"No!"

I laughed. "Why? Do you think they'd storm his house and harm him?"

"Hardly that, but if Glen knows we suspect him—which he'd hear about in ten seconds—he'll lie low for a long time. We need him to act now. Which is why your plan of spreading the word that Heath Richards is almost bankrupt—or will be if something else happens—is perfect," she said.

That was a pretty good idea. "Once Jaxson and I speak with Steve, let's get together and come up with a plan."

She grinned. "I love it. With Drake, right?"

It gave me great joy to see her care about my bestie so much. "Totally."

After we hugged, I rushed off to the office. Jaxson and

Iggy both looked up when I entered. "How's Andorra?"

"Good." I told him what we discussed—minus the part about me questioning whether Iggy was telling the truth.

"We're sure Glen is the guilty party?" he asked.

"Not one-hundred percent confident, which is why I need a favor."

His brows rose. "I'm listening."

"My finger pointing is based on the fact that Glen's hands turned hot when he became angry with Terry so much so that she had blisters on her arm the next day."

"And that led you to conclude that Glen had some kind of spell or curse put on him to rid him of his anger—and that spell failed."

I appreciated that he remembered everything I'd said. "Yes."

"I can see the logic in that. What's the favor?"

"Could you speak with Aaron again to get his take on what happened the day Terry was injured?"

Jaxson paused for a moment. His glance to the side implied he was trying to put the pieces together. "I can do that. I see this going in one of three ways. Aaron will say that Terry was telling the truth, say that she lied, or he plain didn't remember. But...let's suppose he says there were only faint marks on her arm."

"You mean like bruises?"

"Yes. If that's the case, would you say Glen is in the clear?"

I based everything on Glen having the ability to heat his hands. "Probably."

"That would mean that Aaron might have been the arsonist, right?"

We did only have two viable suspects. "I guess. What are you getting at?"

"Is it smart to let Aaron know what we're up to?" he asked.

"I see the conflict here. If Aaron is the arsonist, he would corroborate Terry's story to make us think Glen is guilty, which defeats my plan. What should we do?"

Jaxson gathered me into his arms. "I'll talk to him. I'm pretty good at reading people."

I looked up at him. "You are, and thank you."

"You bet." He gave me a brief kiss.

"I wish Rihanna was here. She'd be able to tell if he was telling the truth."

"I'll be fine. Be back in a jiffy." Jaxson grabbed his phone and keys and left.

I needed a tea—one with lots of sugar. Was I wrong to think Glen was guilty? He had a good motive, but accusing an innocent person was unconscionable. Was it possible Glen couldn't help himself from doing that evil deed? I really knew little about this curse—assuming he'd been affected by one.

I made my drink, and when I returned to the living room, Iggy was on the table. "What do you think, Detective Iggy?"

"I know nothing."

"Since when? You always have an opinion as to who is guilty. You kind of interviewed all of the parties involved."

He lifted his chest. "I did, didn't I?"

"Yes. Who is your number one suspect?"

"Did you ever think it might have been Hugo?"

I stilled. That was ridiculous. "Your good friend, the

gargoyle? He never leaves the store."

"He was a gargoyle on top of the church before Andorra found him. That means he can go outside."

He did have a point. "She had said Hugo transformed into his human form outside of the church—when she was twelve. Why do you think he's guilty? He said he can't shoot fire out of his mouth like some gargoyles can." I sucked in a breath. "You don't think there are other evil gargoyles who can do that, do you?"

Iggy spun around three times and then stopped. "You are so gullible. Hugo wouldn't hurt a fly. I had you going, didn't I?"

I wanted to pick him up and shake him—only I wouldn't. He was too little for handling like that. "You are a little stinker."

"I wanted to lighten the mood."

I sipped my tea. "Fine. You got me. Other than Hugo, who is your top suspect?"

"I don't know anyone that well. Run through all of the potential arsonists again and tell me why you think they might be guilty."

Normally, I might not bother, but it would give me a chance to organize my thoughts. I listed the people, giving their possible motives. "Keep in mind that only Aaron and Christian are warlocks, according to you."

"I never tested that insurance lady."

"I know, but she had nothing to gain by burning the building. Think motive here."

Iggy dropped down on his stomach. "Okay, then Glen."

"Assuming he can set fire to paper with his hands?"

"Yes."

I probably had prejudiced him by what I'd said, but I liked the confirmation. "Let's hope that Jaxson doesn't find out something that totally contradicts this."

We didn't have to wait long before he returned. When Jaxson walked in with a smug look on his face, I knew he'd been victorious. "I trust you learned something."

"Let me get a drink, and I will tell you something you won't believe."

I disliked waiting more than anything, even if it was for only one minute, but I didn't have a choice. Jaxson grabbed a bottle of water and returned. "I spoke with Aaron, and he confirmed that Terry's arm blistered the next day."

Good. "She's sure it was from when Glen grabbed her?"

"Yes, but that in and of itself isn't what is impressive, or rather should I say damaging."

Now he had my undivided attention. "Do tell."

"About a week or so before that incident, Terry and Glen had gone to a drive-thru for some drinks. Terry didn't go into detail about the discussion, but Aaron thinks it was about him trying to get Terry to go out with him. Glen got so mad that when he reached across the backseat of his car, the material caught fire and then set her hair ablaze."

I sucked in a breath. "All by itself?"

"Apparently. It freaked Terry out, but she was a quick thinker. She tossed the soda on it, which put out the fire."

"How did Glen explain it?"

"He said he'd put a protective coating on the seat covers, and when he grabbed it, an ash from the cigarette he was holding must have ignited it. Terry said she was too upset over the stench of her hair to worry about how the fire had started."

"Wow."

"Does this tilt the arsonist theory in Glen's favor or away from him? Personally, I'm leaning toward him. I find it hard to believe an ash would cause a blaze to start so fast," Jaxson said.

"You might be right, but as much as I want to say it was Glen, I'm going to give Christian a call."

"Christian, why?" he asked.

"To triple confirm the story. The whole story seems fishy. If Glen's seat covers caught on fire, wouldn't he have to replace them? Where better than at the garage where he works?"

"He might have ordered a new set online, but sure, give Christian a call. Tell him not to tell Glen that we suspect him. If we don't catch him in the act of trying to set something else on fire, he'll go free."

"That's what worries me." I thought a moment. "Wait a minute."

"What?"

"When Rihanna first spoke with Terry in the library, she read her mind. She said that Terry wasn't telling the whole truth."

"What was she omitting?" Jaxson asked.

"All Rihanna said was that she heard the words *soda* and *flames.*"

He whistled. "Sounds like confirmation to me, but to be sure, go ahead and call Christian. The real question is how did the seat covers catch on fire? Was it due to a cigarette ash or because Glen was angry with Terry? Only she'd know."

"I doubt she'd tell us. I'll call Christian first and see if he can add any information."

Chapter Fourteen

I GOT OFF the phone with Christian and sat next to Jaxson. "Christian confirmed that Glen said the cleaner he used on the car seat must have been defective because when he lit up a cigarette, it went up in flames. Good thing he had a drink handy to put it out."

"Any mention of Terry being in the car at the time?" he asked.

"Nope. Interesting, huh? While it might not stand up in court, Glen is sounding more and more guilty," I said.

"Why not tell the truth? Did he think Christian might mention something to Terry, assuming he ran into her?" he asked.

"Hard to say what Glen was thinking."

"Do we know when this fire occurred?" Jaxson asked. "Before his father lost his job or after?"

"I have no idea. When we see Andorra, we can ask her. She might know, if she's spoken with her friend Sylvia lately."

"Sounds good. When we see Steve, are you going to let him know your theory about Glen?"

I had to think about that. "If we want Steve to watch the building, shouldn't he be aware that Aaron is a warlock and that Glen might be cursed? I'll make sure to explain that I could be wrong."

Jaxson smiled. "Always good to have an out."

I chuckled. "Ready?"

I'm sure Iggy wanted to go with us to the sheriff's department, but it was hard when neither Steve nor Nash could hear him. Before my sassy familiar could ask to join, we left.

Jennifer Larson was at the front desk instead of Pearl, and that worried me a bit. I hoped Bertha had held off telling everyone about this save-Witch's-Cove event until after I'd spoken with the sheriff. The last thing I needed was for Bertha to gather the troops before we were ready. Once Pearl knew of our plan, the whole town would know—including the arsonist.

"Is the sheriff in?" I asked.

"He is."

When we turned to go to his office, who should be in the glassed-in conference room but the gossip queens. Really? "What are my aunt and the other ladies doing here?"

Jennifer smiled. "They are trying to save the town."

Oh, no. This could ruin everything. I turned to Jaxson. "I need to see what they are up to."

"I'm right behind you."

Without stopping to see the sheriff or the deputy, we headed to the conference room. I knocked and entered. "Is this meeting open to anyone?" I asked with as much cheer as I could muster.

"For you two, of course," my aunt said. "Have a seat."

Jaxson and I sat down. "Is this about the fundraiser?" I asked.

Bertha shook her head ever so slightly.

"Fundraiser?" Pearl asked.

Whoops. Me and my big mouth. "It was something I was batting around for…ah…Memorial Day." I cleared my throat. "So, tell me why you are all meeting in secrecy?" *Please let them buy my evasive comment.*

"I was explaining how we believe that the arsonist was targeting poor Mr. Richards and not Frank's store," Bertha said.

"I agree. We can't be certain, though, until we catch him in the act and ask him."

The whole group nodded.

"Who do you suspect, Glinda?" Maude asked.

After learning that Glen had lied about the circumstances regarding his burned slipcovers, I would put my money on Glen. "I can't be certain, but the clues point to Glen Harmony." I held up a hand. "Please don't let that out. If he knows we know, he might go to another town to seek his revenge." I explained that Mr. Richards owned strip malls in other towns.

"Don't you worry," Pearl said. "Mums the word."

Yeah, right. Every inch of her body was comprised of the gossip gene.

I waited for others to comment on my choice of arsonist, but they merely looked at each other, except for Bertha who understood why I picked him.

"I don't know who that is," Miriam said. "Why do you suspect him, dear?"

I laid out the evidence, including his lie about Terry not being in the car when the fire started, and then how he'd touched Terry and burned her. I even explained that

Gertrude, who wasn't there, agreed that Glen could have been cursed. "I have a plan. It starts with all of you telling everyone you see that Heath Richards will have to shut down all of the stores he owns if there is another fire."

"Sounds reasonable," my aunt said.

When no one said anything, I hoped that meant they were all on board.

Dolly sat up straighter. "Wait a minute. Won't that only serve to encourage Glen to start another fire?"

Bertha smiled. "That was what I was about to tell you all before Glinda and Jaxson came in. We need to catch Glen in the act. The problem is manpower." She explained what needed to be done.

Pearl sat back with a self-satisfied look on her face. "We need to start a protect-the-building watch brigade," she said.

"But Steve and Nash are only two people," Miriam said.

"I know, but I bet I could round up twenty people who would be willing to help. I know it might mean we have to stay up at night and wait for this Glen fellow to strike again, but we can't let another building burn." Pearl nodded twice for emphasis.

That was the sweetest thing I'd ever heard come out of her mouth. "That is so generous, but what happens if the arsonist sees you waiting for him? If it is Glen, he's over six feet tall. You could be harmed."

She looked crestfallen. "We would hide."

I looked over at Jaxson. "There has to be a better way."

He sucked in his bottom lip for a moment. "How about if we install security cameras above every entrance or possibly somewhere across the street? If we do, then the ladies can monitor the feed from the comfort of their own homes. The moment they see someone, they could call Steve, Nash, or maybe the fire department."

How did I get so lucky to be with such a smart man? "I really like that idea since it would keep everyone safe, but what if he enters from the back like he did before?"

Jaxson shrugged. "We'll make sure there are lights above each door with a tamperproof cage over the light so he can't bust it. Close by or high above the door will be a camera."

"That sounds awesome. Ladies, what do you think?"

"I can get some of my servers to take a shift," Maude said.

"Great." I turned to Pearl. "We'll need a point person to organize who is on duty and when. Can you do that?"

"Absolutely."

I turned back to Aunt Fern. "I bet Penny and Hunter would be willing to take a shift, as would Andorra and Drake." Penny and I used to waitress together and loved to volunteer for a good cause.

"I'll speak with her," my aunt said.

Even with a lot of people watching, we needed our arsonist to only go into the Hex and Bones store so that Hugo could perform his magic. "You guys are fantastic, but if we are to catch him in the act, we need to lure him into one of the stores where we'll have video cameras recording everything."

"Direct him to my store," Bertha said.

Thank goodness she was in on the plan to use Hugo. "That is awesome."

She waved a hand. "There's less to burn in my store. If he attacked Silas' music store, everything might go up in flames."

"I agree. Okay, ladies, there is a lot of work that still needs to be done in figuring out the logistics, but we've made a great start. Pearl, I'll stop back in one or two days to see how you're coming with your list. In the meantime, Jaxson and I will arrange for surveillance."

"I think the other store owners would pony up for the cameras. After all, their stores are in danger," Dolly said.

"You're right. I'll ask them." I turned to Bertha. "Do you know if Mr. Richards has spoken with them yet?"

Bertha shook her head. "He said he just spoke with Silas, since he's been running the music store for as long as I have."

The rest would be paying a lot more rent, so there might not be a need for Mr. Richards to hound them, yet. "Sounds good. I'll be in touch."

I stood, and Jaxson followed me out. I had so many concerns, but I hadn't wanted to blab about Hugo to these gossip queens. I didn't have a problem letting Steve in on Hugo's new talents however, since he already knew about him from a previous case.

We went to his office, knocked, and entered.

He looked up. "I see you've been stirring the pot, Glinda."

"Because your grandmother and her friends want to save this town?"

He smiled. "Have a seat. Honestly, I'm glad you're here. I'm happy you're not giving up on finding the arsonist."

"I'm not." We sat down. "A lot has happened since we've last seen you."

"I'd love to hear what you've found out." He opened his desk drawer and pulled out his trusty yellow pad.

"As I've mentioned, we believe magic is involved."

"That is a strong possibility. Any idea who might be responsible?" he asked.

"Yes." I went through how Iggy tested each person. "The only one who tested positive—if that is the right way of looking at it—was Aaron Reed."

"The firefighter, Aaron Reed?"

I didn't think there were two Aaron Reeds in Witch's Cove, especially two who were firefighters. "Yes, but I don't think he's guilty."

Steve's brows rose. "Now you have me even more curious."

I explained about Glen's hot hands—including how he burned Terry's arm and set his car seat on fire. "I even confirmed with Christian that his car slipcovers had to be replaced. I also spoke with Gertrude, and she believes someone put a spell or curse on Glen, possibly to curb his anger."

Steve whistled. "That is hard to digest. At the moment, you think Glen Harmony is guilty. Why would he burn down the bookstore?"

I went through the whole thing about how Heath Richards had to shut down a mall in Summertime. "Glen's dad lost his job because of that closure."

"That's a good enough motive, I guess." He tapped his pencil on the pad. "Considering I have a group of women in my conference room, I have the sense that there is more to the story."

"There is. We want them to spread the word that Heath Richards will have to shut down this row of stores if he has another fire."

As expected, Steve's brows pinched. "That's asking our arsonist to strike again."

"Yes, which is our plan."

"*Our* plan?"

I don't know why he was being so fussy. If magic was involved, Jaxson and I had to be on board. "Bertha and I kind of came up with an idea. Okay, in truth, Iggy helped. It involves Hugo." I detailed what he suggested.

"This statue turned human can do that?"

I explained how he'd teleported next to me, and when he touched my shoulder, I couldn't move. "If we can catch Glen in the act of setting the fire, Hugo will do his thing, which is to encase Glen's hands in some kind of magical ice. He seems to think that by the time the stuff melts, the curse will be broken."

"Wouldn't that give Glen frostbite? He could lose the use of his hands," Steve asked.

"I'll double check with Hugo, but he said it was *magical* ice."

"Fine. There are several stores in this strip," Steve said. "Who's to say Glen, or whoever is guilty, will chose Hex and Bones?"

Jaxson touched my arm. He explained about the security cameras and how the feed would be sent to several places, each manned by someone Pearl chooses.

"You're putting my grandmother in charge of this?"

"Only partially. I'll check on the list."

"What if they see someone?" Steve asked.

I explained that they would call him, Nash, or the fire department. "I'll let you work that out with the volunteers."

"That's all well and good, but I still don't see how you plan on making sure this person goes to the Hex and Bones store and not to the music store, for example. Seems to me, burning a store with sheet music would be easier than a store that sells clothes and occult paraphernalia."

I looked over at Jaxson. When he didn't answer, I winged it. "We could put security gates over all of the back doors but leave the one to the Hex and Bones ajar. He'll think it is a mistake. Quite honestly, if the arsonist's goal is to hurt Heath Richards, Glen shouldn't care which place he burns down."

"Sounds reasonable. He entered through the back before."

"If we add additional light in the front, as well as very prominent cameras, it should prompt him to go to the back," Jaxson said.

Steve stared at me for a bit. "I have to say, I am impressed."

Wow. A compliment from Sheriff Steve Rocker. "Thank you. And once we have him in custody, I'm going to ask the women if they'll help me with a fundraiser." I explained what that would entail. "I hope I have your support."

"By all means. I will speak with the mayor to make sure we dot our i's and cross our t's."

"I appreciate it."

After we discussed the logistics a bit more, we left. "We should probably touch base with the rest of the shop owners to let them know what we're planning," I said.

"Good thinking. I imagine they might be a little suspicious if we install cameras on the front and back of their businesses without telling them why."

"Yes, and I'm hoping they might volunteer to take a shift

watching the camera feed. I will suggest they take home anything really valuable," I said.

"Silas might want to rent a storage unit for the month. Those pianos and some of those guitars aren't cheap."

"You're right about that. Who are you going to call about installing the security equipment on these stores? We'll have to get on it ASAP. Once the gossip queens tell Witch's Cove about the possible closing of the stores on the main street, no telling how long it will take before Glen hears about it."

"I have a friend in the security business, but I think we should also use Christian."

"Why?"

Chapter Fifteen

"WATCHING A TELEVISION screen all day that only shows the back of a building can get really boring," Jaxson said as he booted up his office computer.

"I know, but these volunteers know how important it is to stay focused."

"I'm sure they do, but it would help if Christian can give us a heads up if Glen mentions anything about Heath Richards. I doubt he'll strike in the middle of the day, but it might help us learn when Glen plans on setting the fire."

"That's a great idea. Do you want me to ask him?"

"No, I'll do it. I have to go out and get the security stuff set up anyway," he said.

"I know I don't need to tell you, but please emphasize the need to do this quickly. In the meantime, I'll make my rounds and talk to the owners."

"Good. Between the two of us, we'll get everyone ready and on board."

"Can I come?" Iggy asked. "I'm bored."

"How about I let you chat with Hugo while I speak with the other owners?"

"That's a good plan. Hugo and I will figure out how we want this sting operation to go down."

I wasn't sure how to respond. "Are you in charge now?"

"Kind of. Andorra and I are the only ones who can talk to Hugo. Without him, none of this works."

"You have a point." I was pleased that my familiar was so willing to help. "Let's go see Hugo then."

When we entered the store, both Andorra and Elizabeth were there, but I didn't see Bertha. I suspected she might be doing some planning with the gossip queens.

"I didn't expect you back here so soon," Andorra said.

I opened my purse. "I'm delivering Iggy, assuming you don't mind him and Hugo having a play date."

She laughed. "I love it. Anything new?"

She must not have spoken with her grandmother yet, so I told her about the meeting.

"That's super that the women are going to organize the surveillance."

"It is. Jaxson is out now rounding up the equipment. I'm hoping he can get them to install everything by tomorrow. Then the women can spread the word that if there is another fire, Heath Richards will be ruined."

She whistled. "This is happening fast."

"I hope Hugo is up for it."

"He will be."

"Not that this is critical information, but I was wondering if your friend Sylvia might know whether Terry was burned before or after Glen's father's business was shut down?"

"I can call her."

"That would be great."

"Let's do this in the back room."

I needed to take Iggy back there anyway. "Could you also

ask her if Glen was always an angry guy?"

"Sure."

While I reunited the two friends, Andorra made the call. I wasn't sure why Sylvia would know, but maybe she would call Terry to find out.

They spoke for a few minutes, and then Andorra hung up. "Seems as if Terry likes to spill her guts to her bestie. Yes, Glen has anger issues. So much so, that he sought treatment, but Terry said nothing seemed to work. After his father's dry cleaners closed, he began to drink, and Glen kind of lost it. That was when she started seeing Aaron."

I always hated to hear about relationships that failed. "That all seems to fit. I wonder who he saw for treatment? More specifically if traditional treatment didn't work, did he try a witch to help him?"

Her eyes widened. "I have no idea, but it sounds plausible. Should I ask Terry—or rather have Sylvia ask her?"

I had to think about that. "Better not. If Glen finds out we are inquiring about him, things could get messed up."

She nodded. "Good thinking. What's next on the plan?"

"I need to talk to the other owners. I fear that Silas Adams might be trouble."

"Why? He should be super happy that you guys are going to set up surveillance."

I hoped she was right. "I know, but Silas can be a curmudgeon at times."

"Then good luck. Iggy can stay here for as long as you like."

I hugged her. "Thanks."

After I told Iggy I would be back shortly, and then him

telling me to take my time, I headed out. Sometimes, I wondered if he cared that I had been the one to find him that day in the forest.

Now wasn't the time to dwell on that. At least he wasn't complaining, which was a good thing. I went next door to the music shop and found Silas packing up some sheet music.

He looked up. "We're closed. Didn't you see the sign?"

Yes, Mr. Friendly, I did. "I needed to talk to you about the fire at the bookstore."

He continued packing. "What about it? Come to tell me I might be next? I already figured that out."

I didn't expect that. "Why is that?"

"That Richards kid stopped by to tell me that he needs to raise the rent, or he'll be forced to close this strip of stores."

I wasn't sure what Silas planned to do about it. "Are you going to pay more?"

"Nope."

"You're okay if he closes?"

"Yup."

This was going to be a harder sell than I thought. "Are you going to sell your inventory and retire?"

He stopped packing. "What's it to you?"

Someone got up on the wrong side of the bed. "I'm trying to prevent these stores from shutting down, which is why Jaxson Harrison, my partner, is out buying security cameras to put outside of each store. We have a bunch of volunteers willing to watch the feeds in case the arsonist shows up. We can't afford to have even one more fire."

"That's why I'm packing."

"Are you packing to get ready to sell, or are you packing

to prevent losing inventory in case there is a fire?"

He looked up at me. Maybe it was the light, but Silas looked a lot older than a few months ago. I wouldn't be surprised if he wasn't sleeping.

"Maybe a little of both." He coughed.

"Are you okay?"

"Yeah. I haven't slept much since the fire. I keep thinking I might lose everything. I don't think Kathy would survive if we lost the store."

"I understand." I wanted to take a chance on something. I pulled out my phone and located a picture of Glen Harmony on social media. I held the phone up to him. "Have you ever seen this young man before?"

Silas took the phone and squinted. "Came in a few weeks ago asking about a guitar."

As much as I didn't want to accuse anyone without proof, the facts were building against Glen Harmony. "It's possible, Glen was here to scope out the place."

It took Silas a minute to understand. "You think he'll hit this place next?"

"I'm hoping not." I explained about putting security gates on the back of each door.

"I heard the arsonist was able to break the lock in the bookstore. If he's good enough, I bet he can get through any security door."

I hoped that wasn't true. "We're going to leave one door unlocked. We want him to go into one store—the Hex and Bones—where we will capture him."

"What does Bertha say about that?"

I liked that he sounded protective of her. "She offered to

have it at her store. Our arsonist seems to set fire to paper products, and Bertha has a lot of books that contain spells."

I'd have to suggest she put them in a very safe place. It would be terrible if those went up in flames.

"I see. I'll make sure to store my sheet music back at the house, but I plan on sleeping in the back room at night."

"I don't think that is wise." Silas was quite old and no match for the much younger Glen.

"Why?"

I couldn't tell him the real reason. "We think he's violent."

"Oh."

"What you can do to help is talk to Pearl about volunteering to watch the security cameras for a few hours. If you see anyone checking out the stores, call the sheriff's department."

He went back to repacking his boxes. "I'll think about it."

I would bring up the idea of him chipping in for the security cameras and the doors later. Silas seemed to be struggling with the idea of an arsonist as it was.

"Thank you."

He didn't answer, so I left. I was pleased that he was at least worried and willing to mitigate the damage by packing his valuables should Glen decide to set fire to his store. Once we had the surveillance in place, I found it hard to believe that the arsonist would be able to do much damage.

I spoke to the other owners, all of whom were very supportive, especially the pharmacy. Their security seemed to be top-notch so that was one less place we'd have to worry about.

When I returned to Hex and Bones, Bertha was there. "How did the rest of the meeting go?" I asked.

"Good. I think we have things covered. It will be quite the chore for the installer to teach the women how to monitor the feed, though, but we'll figure it out."

I smiled. "Jaxson will help. I'm sure he can get them up to speed in no time." Though it could take him days, depending on the number of volunteers.

"I'm sure he can. You're lucky to have such a great guy."

My heart fluttered. "I am." I looked over at the pile of books on the side table. "I know that Hugo will be able to prevent Glen from doing much damage, but we might have to let him set something on fire in order to charge him with arson."

Bertha's face paled. "I never thought of that. Otherwise, he'd be charged with breaking and entering."

"Exactly. Not only that, what if Hugo doesn't hear him come in?"

"He will. He can sense danger. I don't know how, but that shouldn't be a problem."

"I hope so." I nodded to the books on the table. "Those spell books are irreplaceable. Do you think you could maybe store them in the back room for a few days?"

Bertha let out a long breath. "That is a great idea. Want to help?"

I grinned. "I'd love to." I would have suggested we ask Hugo to give us a hand, but I wasn't sure if she and her granddaughters wanted him to be walking around in view of the public. If anyone asked him a question and he didn't answer, it might upset some people.

For the next ten minutes, we carried the spell books to the back. "Maybe you can put a cloth over them just in case Glen wanders back here."

"Hugo won't let anything happen to them," Iggy piped up.

Whoops. I'd forgotten he was even back here. "Tell Hugo thank you. These are very important books to Bertha and the community."

I would have to consult with Andorra to instruct Hugo not to ice Glen's hands too soon. "Can Hugo cloak himself?" I asked to no one in particular.

I didn't need Iggy to answer. One minute Hugo was there and the next he wasn't. He could have teleported into the main room, but I had the sense he hadn't.

"Does that answer your question?" my cute familiar said.

"Yes, thank you, Hugo. You can uncloak."

He did and was right where I'd last seen him. Knowing he had that talent would help us figure out how this whole capture-Glen event would go down.

I turned to Bertha. "Do you think Pearl will be ready tomorrow with the list of volunteers?"

"We've all been tasked with finding five people, so yes. I may ask Elizabeth to coordinate the schedule. I don't think that's Pearl's forte."

"Maybe not. I'm hoping tomorrow the cameras will be installed. Jaxson said he'd place a video camera inside this store, so we can record what is going on."

"I had planned to have cameras installed, but I was hesitating because of what people might do if they saw Hugo."

I hadn't thought of that. "If we need to use the video in a court of law, perhaps we'll cut it off right after Glen sets something on fire. We don't need the world to see Hugo encasing Glen's hands in magical ice either."

Her eyes lit up. "Perfect. I have an idea. How about if I buy some paper and put it on that front table? The arsonist will hopefully choose that to set on fire. The counter might burn, but I'm willing to chance it."

"That's a great idea. Can Hugo put out a fire?" That was probably a dumb question. If he could ice hands, he could ice flames.

"Hugo can do anything," Iggy said.

Oh, boy. Someone had hero worship.

Chapter Sixteen

IGGY AND I returned to the office, and it wasn't long before Jaxson showed up. His success at finding someone willing and able to install all of the surveillance equipment was key to catching our arsonist.

"So?" I asked.

Jaxson held up a hand. "Good news and maybe not such good news."

"I'm listening." I looked down at Iggy. "Considering my familiar is our detective, he'll need to be able to relay everything to Hugo."

"Of course. The security doors will be installed later today."

"Excellent. And the not such good news?"

"Partially good and partially not good. Abe will be installing the cameras both in the front and in the back this afternoon, and Chuck will add additional lights at the same time."

Why did he think that wasn't good news? "I'm impressed."

"Here's the thing. I know we wanted our volunteers to be able to watch the security feed from their homes, but that is not possible. The best these guys can do in the allotted time is set up the monitors in the sheriff's department glassed-in room." He held up a hand. "Don't worry. I stopped by and told Steve about the change in plan, and he is fine with it."

"I guess that means our volunteers will have to be at the office to view what's happening twenty-four seven. That could be inconvenient for many." This was getting more and more complicated.

"It could. I told Pearl what needs to happen, so she's up to speed. She told me she'll let everyone know," he said. "Now that I think about it, though, we probably can get away with not having someone monitor the feed during the day. There's no way our arsonist can get in and out during business hours without the owners noticing," Jaxson said.

"You're right. We'll put them on high alert, though. If their back doors are locked, they should be good."

"We'll ask Bertha to unlock hers once we're all set up, and the gossip queens have done their job."

"This seems like it just might work." I needed to think of any other issues that might pop up. "Jennifer Larson leaves at around two in the morning. The sheriff department doors are locked after that. How are people going to get inside?"

Jaxson let out a self-satisfied sigh. "I got you covered. Or rather, Nash says he'll have that covered. What that means exactly, I don't know. Maybe he'll be there to open the doors at two or someone else will. Regardless, the office will be open."

Goose bumps raced up my arms. "I can't believe you got that together so fast."

He grinned. "There's nothing I can't do, pink lady." He tapped my nose.

"You can't talk to Hugo like I can," Iggy chimed in, causing both of us to laugh.

"You are right about that, Iggy." I turned back to Jaxson. "Having the volunteers monitor the cameras is all well and good, but what happens when our arsonist finds that the Hex and Bones back door is open, and he walks into our trap? I'm a little fuzzy on the procedure."

"Iggy?" Jaxson asked. "Did Hugo tell you his plan?"

"When he hears anyone coming in, Hugo will cloak himself and follow the arsonist around."

I waited for him to add something more than I already knew. "Does he understand when he's supposed to ice the man's hands?"

"Yes. As soon as the guy heats up his hands and lights something on fire, Hugo will put out the fire and then ice Glen's hands. The guy won't know what hit him."

I hoped Hugo was good at keeping cloaked. Since he didn't eat or sleep, he might not have infinite energy—but I hoped I was wrong. "Sounds perfect." I turned to Jaxson. "We good then?"

"There is one more thing that has to be done that I will deal with shortly."

"Which is?" I asked.

"I have to get someone to install one or two video cameras inside each of the stores if there aren't any already. But my biggest worry is that Glen will wait days or weeks before he strikes again."

"I disagree. Once the gossip queens spread the news that one more fire will finish Mr. Richards for good, Glen won't wait very long. He'll want to hurt Heath as quickly and as hard as possible."

Jaxson crossed his fingers, something he'd picked up from me. "I have to hand it to you, Glinda, it's a good plan. I hope you are right."

"Assuming Hugo does what he claims, it is a great plan, but I feel like I'm not doing enough."

Jaxson's eyes widened. "What do you mean? You figured most things out."

"I know, but Hugo is doing all of the magic."

"Come on. You figured out that Glen wasn't a warlock but that he might have had a spell put on him. That takes a magical mind to do that."

"Actually, you thought of it."

Iggy looked up at me and then tapped my hand to get my attention. "Yes?" I asked.

"Jaxson is right. Just because Hugo is going to freeze Glen's hands doesn't mean you couldn't have learned how to do it."

My heart melted at the sentiment. "I'm not sure that's true, but thank you. Maybe I should learn how to do it just in case Hugo fails."

"He won't fail," Iggy said. I liked his confidence.

"I'll see if I have time to learn it." Jaxson seemed to be fighting a smile. "What's funny?"

"I think it's cute that you are having a hard time giving up your witch power to a gargoyle."

"If you're saying I like to be in control, then you'd be right. A lot is at stake here."

"I know, maybe more than any other case we've worked on," Jaxson said.

"That's because the whole town is in danger of losing its main set of storefronts."

"Let's hope it doesn't come to it. You do have that awesome fundraiser, remember?"

So much to do. So little time. "Don't remind me."

"What if Glen isn't the arsonist?" Iggy asked.

My stomach churned at that thought. Our plan was based on it. "What do you mean?"

"I really like Aaron," Iggy said, "but what if he is guilty and not Glen?"

I looked over at Jaxson and shrugged. "It is possible. What do you think? Does it make any difference? Hugo will still freeze the arsonist's hands."

"You said the freezing was to cancel a curse. Would a warlock be cursed?"

This was terrible. "Maybe not."

"In case it is Aaron, which I sincerely doubt it is, how about I ask Ian to keep an eye on him?"

"You always come up with the answers," I said. "In either case, it might be wise to let Hugo know about the possible change. He could still put the fire out and stun Aaron long enough for Steve to arrest him."

"Sounds good, but there is something we can do to see if Glen was our arsonist."

"What are you talking about?"

"How do we know that Glen hasn't set other things on fire? Maybe he found out he had powers and wanted to test them out. These fires could have nothing to do with Heath Richards and everything to do with Glen's new abilities."

I couldn't connect the dots. "Suppose you learn he's set

other fires. How does that help us?"

"You love patterns. Maybe there is a time of day or night that he likes to do his test runs. He burned the bookstore at around three in the morning. It would be convenient if we knew when he typically strikes."

"I'd feel better about dismissing people during the day if we knew that. How can you find out?"

"I could search the Internet for fires, but I'm betting Ian Silver would know, or the fire chief for that matter."

"That's a good plan."

"I'll speak with him. And you?" he asked.

"I need to stop at the sheriff's office for a couple of reasons. I'm betting Pearl is chomping at the bit to tell the world about our fundraiser—assuming she learned about it—and I need to ask her to hold off for a little longer."

"She didn't mention it to me, and I just saw her."

That was good. "Secondly, what do you think about me asking Steve to find people to follow Glen around for a few days?"

"I like it. Just don't suggest it to Rihanna. She'll want to do it."

"Trust me. I won't." I loved my eighteen-year old cousin, but I didn't need her involved with someone as powerful as Glen. It didn't matter she was a strong witch herself. "Lastly, I'd love to see if Steve or Nash could be in the Hex and Bones when Glen shows up."

"I'm not sure how you can accomplish that, but give it a try." Jaxson leaned over and kissed my forehead. "If anyone can figure it out, it's you."

"Aw, thank you."

"I gotta go," he said.

"See you."

Once Jaxson left, I turned to Iggy. "Do you want to fill Hugo in on what we're doing? I know he has a plan, but maybe you'd like to go over it again with him, and then warn him that it could be someone other than Glen who shows up."

He did a circle dance. "Yes. I'll give him the entire lowdown."

I smiled. "You do that. Speaking of friends, have you even seen Aimee today?" At one time, all he could think about was his cat girlfriend.

"No, I've been kind of busy."

This was a good opportunity to explain about relationships—not that he'd listen. Iggy had a mind of his own. "Even though you are busy, you have to let Aimee know that you are thinking of her."

He tilted his head, but I couldn't decode what that meant. "Are we going to see Hugo or not?"

"We are." I guess the topic of relationships didn't interest him today.

I hoped that Bertha, Andorra, and Elizabeth didn't think I was using them as babysitters since Iggy could take care of himself. After putting Iggy in my purse, we left. Once inside the apothecary, I found Bertha. Elizabeth was with a customer at the counter, and Andorra wasn't there. I really should get their work schedules.

"Glinda, have you learned anything?" Bertha asked.

"I have."

She must have read my mind, because she turned around and headed into the back room. I joined her and then let Iggy out. Naturally, he raced up to Hugo. If I wasn't mistaken, it looked as if he smiled.

"The security gate, cameras, lights, and video camera for inside, should be installed today." I explained that everyone needed to view the feed from the sheriff's office.

"That was fast, but it might be more fun to have everyone in one spot anyway."

I loved her attitude. "I hope so."

"Oh, and be sure to tell me the cost. I want to pay for it all," Bertha said.

"You don't have to do that—at least not all of it. Many of the other owners have agreed to chip in, and once we have our fundraiser, I'm sure you'll be reimbursed."

"I'm good either way. What do you need me to do?"

That was a good question. "Nothing at the moment. You've removed the important paper products from view. I'm going to talk with Pearl about scheduling and see if Steve can be here when Glen comes to do his thing. The problem is that we don't know when he plans to show, which is why Jaxson is going to talk with Christian to see about Glen's work schedule."

Bertha hugged me. "You are the best."

"You are sweet." I looked over at Iggy. "You good to stay here for a bit while I talk to Pearl?"

"I can spend the night."

"That's not going to happen."

Bertha smiled. "Don't worry, I'll watch him."

"If he gives you any trouble, call me."

"He'll be fine."

Knowing Bertha had everything under control, I left to

speak with Pearl. Jaxson had talked to Steve about the surveillance, but I needed to be sure that Pearl understood everything. Also, finding people to watch the feed from say two to four in the morning would be difficult. While it would be difficult to stay awake, I wanted to volunteer, and hopefully, Jaxson would join me.

To my delight, Pearl had been busy baking cookies again. The office smelled of chocolate. I don't know how she managed not to eat all of them. I know I would have.

I suspected this new batch was to lure people into volunteering their time. "Hey, Pearl, how is the list coming?"

She shook her head. "It was great until Jaxson told us the feed couldn't be streamed to people's homes."

"I know it's a setback, but hopefully, Glen won't wait long once we have everything in place, and you spread the word about Mr. Richards' impending demise."

A sparkle came to her eye. "Don't you worry about spreading that rumor. It will be my pleasure."

I had no doubt of that. "Do you need help with the scheduling?"

"I think I'm good. I'm calling everyone again to say they have to come here. What day will we start?"

I had to do some mental work. "If you can get the word out tomorrow afternoon, I'd say we should start tomorrow evening. I can take the late shift from two to four."

Her shoulders sagged. "You are an angel. No one wanted that time. Everyone I know works."

I worked, too, but at least I could set my own hours. "See you tomorrow then."

"I'll bake cookies. Chocolate chip?"

Be still my beating heart. "That would be awesome."

I hoped that someone would be here to show me what to do if Jaxson didn't join me. He was a whiz at the computer stuff.

"I need to speak with Steve for a moment," I said.

"Sure, you know where he works." Pearl grinned.

I passed by Nash's empty desk. Someday, I'd ask Steve why Nash was usually the one to run around and not him, but I didn't want him to think I was complaining. I liked having access to Steve whenever I needed him.

I knocked and entered. He looked up and smiled. "How's the sting operation coming?"

"Good." I pulled up a chair and detailed what was going on. I even mentioned that it was possible that Aaron was guilty. "Jaxson is asking Ian to keep an eye on him." It looked as if the sheriff was having a hard time containing a smile. "You already did that, didn't you?"

"Yes, ma'am."

"Do you have someone assigned to watch Glen, too?" I bet he didn't.

"I see you are still doubting my abilities. Misty volunteered some of her men to watch him. You said you think he might strike as early as tomorrow night, is that right?"

Wow. I was impressed that he was on top of things. "Yes."

"We will have him watched then. For how long, I can't promise, but at least for a few days."

"That's good enough. Thank you." Now for the hard part. "I wish we could clone you."

"Why?"

"It would be perfect if when the arsonist showed up at the

Hex and Bones, you were already there, waiting for him."

He chuckled. "I'll work on it, but I might need a little magic to help with the duplication process."

I was glad he could joke at a time like this. "I'll see what I can do on my end."

After I left, I headed back to Hex and Bones. Hopefully, Detective Iggy wouldn't put up too much of a fuss that he had to leave.

No surprise, Iggy was in the back with Hugo. "It's time to go, Iggy."

He didn't move for a moment. I assumed he was conversing with his friend. Iggy nodded and then crawled over to me. "I'm starving."

"Hello, to you, too."

"Hi, but do you have anything to eat back at the office?"

"Maybe." I stuffed him in my purse, not in the mood to deal with him right now. I had a lot on my mind.

When we entered the office, Jaxson was there, causing relief to pour through me. I knew I'd get no backtalk from him. "Everything work out?"

"Kind of."

Chapter Seventeen

KIND OF WORKED out? "Care to explain what you mean?"
"Sure. While Glen didn't even bring up Heath Richards' name, in any context, Glen's been acting a bit strange," Jaxson said.

"Strange how?" I asked.

"Christian just said different."

"Good to know. Perhaps Glen is preoccupied with trying to plan his next move, which would account for his strange behavior."

"That's a possibility."

I placed my purse on the floor, and Iggy crawled out. He looked up at me with those wide eyes, not saying a word. He kept quiet, probably because he could sense he'd pushed me too far. I knew what he wanted, and if he hadn't been so cute, I wouldn't have relented. "Let me see what I have for you to eat," I told him.

"Thank you."

I raised a brow, pleased he didn't act like he'd won. I found some lettuce in the refrigerator, placed it on a plate, and carried it out to him. "Here ya go."

"Yum."

Part of me was surprised he didn't complain that it wasn't

flowers and the rest of me was very happy he seemed almost appreciative. I sat next to Jaxson. "Guess what? Steve has set up surveillance for Glen."

He hissed in a breath. "That will take a lot of manpower."

I nodded. "Misty Willows and her officers offered to help. Glen won't recognize any of them."

"Perfect. Actually, Christian volunteered to follow him, but I told him if he—or I—were caught, it would be game over."

"I totally agree. We have to keep an eye on him, because it's not like the sheriff can catch him with a can of gas or anything."

"Very true."

"By the way, I volunteered to take the two to four shift starting tomorrow," I said.

Jaxson dipped his chin. "In the morning?"

"Yes. We agreed we didn't need to man the feed during the day."

"Want company?"

He was the best. "Absolutely. When will you know when all the cameras are set up and the doors are installed?" If the cameras weren't in place, there would be nothing to see.

"I got it covered." He looked at his phone. "In fact, I just received a text from Abe. Cameras are all set. Maybe in a few hours we can walk across the street and make sure everything else is good to go. I want to check out the clarity of the feed, too."

I hugged him. "What would I do without you?"

"I hope you never find out."

"I CAN'T BELIEVE everything came together so quickly," I said.

It took two days of hard work, but that was fast considering all that Jaxson had accomplished. I think within minutes of Pearl and her team spreading the word that Heath Richards might have to shut down the whole strip of stores that even I'd heard about it. Go, gossip ladies.

"It might look that way, but installing the cameras both inside and out as well as putting up the security doors wasn't easy."

"I know. I still think we should have shown a picture of Glen to the other owners. If Glen was scoping out the music store, he might have stopped in at the yarn shop, the pharmacy, or even Hex and Bones."

"Maybe, but I know what it's like to be falsely accused. If Glen is innocent, it might ruin his life."

I suppose if Ian Silver had learned that Glen had set other fires, Jaxson might have gone along with my idea. I was still convinced Glen would have tried out his powers in some location. It just might not have happened in or around Witch's Cove. "I guess."

It was three in the morning, and Jaxson and I were sitting in the sheriff's glass-enclosed room watching multiple feeds of both the front and back of the stores. I won't lie. It was boring. If I didn't have my partner with me, I might have dozed off—or played solitaire on my phone for the two hours, missing any action that happened.

I munched on a cookie that Pearl had graciously left us. I was lost in my own thoughts when Jaxson nudged me.

"Glinda, look, someone is coming, and he's on a bike."

I stiffened, leaned closer to the screen, and squinted. "Who is it? Glen?"

"I can't tell. He's wearing a hoodie."

"He's stopping and looking around." *Please look up at the camera so we can get a shot of your face.*

"Good. He's testing the back doors," Jaxson commented.

I polished off the cookie. "Should we call Steve?"

"He's already in the store."

"Why didn't you tell me?" I know he said he'd try to be there—after he cloned himself—but I honestly hadn't expected him to spend the night or anything.

"I thought you'd be less worried."

That made no sense, but I was too intrigued to see what this person was going to do to ask Jaxson why he thought I'd worry. The hooded man tugged on each door, found it locked, and moved on. "Does he really think one of them will be open?"

"One is unlocked."

"I know, but I would think he'd know which store he wanted to target beforehand and have brought some tools to get in the back."

"The security doors weren't there the last time he burned the bookstore."

Jaxson was always thinking. Instinctively, I grabbed his arm. "He's at Hex and Bones. This is it."

The man pulled open the security door and then closed it. It was as if he was satisfied he could get in whenever he wanted—or else he spotted the security cameras. He returned to his bike and left. "What was up with that?"

Jaxson said nothing for a moment. "I don't think that was Glen."

"How could you tell? He kept his head down the whole time."

"How tall is Glen?" he asked.

"At least six feet."

"Exactly. This person was a lot shorter and did not have the broad shoulders like Glen does."

Darn. He was right. "This person could have been some random thief and not the arsonist."

"Possibly, but the timing seems too coincidental. I'm texting Steve to let him know what happened in case this person returns."

A minute later, Steve poked his head out the back, looked around, and gave us a thumbs up. He then returned inside. "How many days does he plan on keeping this up?" I asked.

"Bertha fixed up a cot for him in the back. Hugo will wake him if he hears anything so Steve should be able to get some shuteye."

"I'll be curious to see if Hugo woke up Steve before you texted him."

Jaxson rubbed my arm. "You need to trust Hugo. You trust Iggy to do some pretty impressive work."

"I do. You're right. I'm a little on edge."

"Turn your chair around."

"Why?" I asked.

He chuckled. "Because I asked you to?"

When he dipped his chin, I did as he asked. The moment his hands began to rub my shoulders, I fell more in love with him. Jaxson always put me first. I sighed. "I needed this."

"I know. Don't worry. We'll catch whoever it is."

I loved his certainty. "Considering we have most of the town witches on our side, I hope you are right."

When I almost fell asleep due to his wonderful massage, I had to ask him to stop. "I don't think you want to have to carry me home."

"I suppose those steps would be tricky what with you banging your head and feet against the handrail on the way up."

Jaxson had the best sense of humor. We finished out our shift, but we couldn't leave until after one of the workers from the Bubbling Cauldron took over. Jaxson gave her a quick rundown on how to view the cameras and what to do if she spotted anyone.

"I got this," she said.

Naturally, Jaxson walked me back to my house and kissed me goodnight. I was tempted to tell him to spend the night, but he didn't have any of his stuff with him. At some point, we'd have to talk about being together permanently. Yikes, that word kind of scared me.

"Sleep in as much as you want," I said.

"Thanks, boss."

"Sorry." We were equal business partners. "If you get in before me and learn something, call."

"And chance your wrath because I woke you up? No, thank you." Jaxson tapped my nose to indicate he was kidding.

"Funny man. See you tomorrow—or rather later today."

As much as I would have liked to head straight to bed, Iggy would want a rundown of the evening's events. When I stepped inside, my familiar cracked open an eye and closed it again. So much for him wanting to be in the know. That worked for me. I was dead tired.

I managed to put on my pajamas and fall into bed without incident. When I awoke, it was close to noon. Yikes.

"About time you woke up," Iggy said. "I guess nothing happened?"

He almost sounded happy. "Actually, someone did show up."

"Why didn't you tell me?"

"You were almost comatose when I came home."

"I guess," he said. "Was it Glen?"

"We couldn't tell." I explained the series of events. "It might have been a kid wondering why there was something new installed."

"Why don't you get Rihanna to touch the door handle. She might see an image."

His comment stunned me. "Why didn't I think of that. It's genius."

If Iggy could have, he would have tilted his head back and laughed. "How quickly you forget I'm Detective Iggy."

Gone was the time of him being humble. "Yes, you are. I need to change, grab something to eat, and get to work. Are you coming?"

"Yes, but I'd like you to drop me off at Hex and Bones," he said.

"Because?"

He blinked a few times—his way of rolling his eyes. "I need to hear what Hugo knows. He was there, you know."

I was there, too, kind of, but Hugo could have sensed

something. "I'll drop you off first then."

"Thank you."

I changed and then texted Jaxson. I would have called, but I didn't want to wake him up in case he was still asleep. He texted me right back, mentioning he'd been at the office for over an hour already. Over achiever.

I called him since I wasn't good at using my thumbs to text. "Hey. Have you had breakfast?"

"No, I was waiting for you," he said.

"Super. I need to drop Iggy off to see Hugo, and then I'll come up to the office."

"Perfect."

I turned to my familiar. "Come on, you."

After placing him in my bag, I walked over to the Hex and Bones. All three women were there. Most likely they wanted to make sure no one snuck in the back during the day.

Bertha came up to me. "I heard we had someone interested in my back door."

I placed Iggy on the floor and let him do his thing. "Yes. I'm going to have Rihanna touch the knob to see if she can get a read off of it."

Bertha clamped a hand over her mouth. "I already touched it. I'm sorry. The sheriff did, too. He was probably looking for clues or something."

I would have thought he'd want to run fingerprints on the handle. "This guy touched all of the doors. I'm guessing it was to see if any of them were open. We'll have to wait and see what she can sense."

Bertha's shoulders relaxed. "Good."

"How was Steve this morning?" I had to assume Bertha

came in bright and early and found him there.

"He said he slept until Hugo woke him up when he heard someone out back."

"That makes me feel better that Hugo wasn't asleep on the job, so to speak, even though I know he doesn't actually sleep." I was babbling. "I'm going to go, but I'll be back with Rihanna as soon as she returns from school. I hope you don't mind if Iggy keeps Hugo company?"

"No, dear. Hugo thinks the world of your little familiar. Those two have really bonded."

I smiled. "Yes, they have."

I waved goodbye to Elizabeth and Andorra, both of whom were with customers. I rushed out and went to the office. When I stepped inside, it was as if I'd left my worries at the doorstep. If there was anything I couldn't figure out, Jaxson was there to help.

He pushed back his chair. "Iggy is happy with his new friend?"

"Yes. I'm hoping Hugo will tell us something."

He snatched up his keys, wallet, and phone. "Let's grab some grub."

"Before we go, we should decide if it is smart to let the world know that someone tried to break into the stores last night."

"I've been thinking about that. I don't think the person was trying to break in. I don't recall that he even tested the inside doorknob—just the security door."

"Why come then, if not to steal?"

"To scope it out, maybe?" he suggested.

I had to think about that. "Yes. He could have shown up

to see what tools his accomplice might need in order to break in."

"If Glen is involved, he'd know what tools were needed."

I snapped my fingers. "Maybe he was there to see if there were any alarms."

Jaxson grinned. "Bingo. As long as we don't question this person, his partner will think it is safe to return."

"Why do I get the sense you know who this person might be?"

"I'm not saying until after Rihanna does her thing, but I'll write it down first, so you don't think I'm making it up."

"Deal."

Chapter Eighteen

JAXSON AND I headed out to Dolly's Spellbound Diner. If we'd eaten at the Tiki Hut, Aunt Fern would have grilled me mercilessly, and I wouldn't have been able to keep from telling her about our plan to catch this guy. And if that were to happen, she might leak it to the other gossip queens. Not that Dolly wouldn't tell the world, but I trusted myself more not to say anything to her.

Even though it was almost lunchtime, we found a booth. I looked around for Dolly but didn't spot her. It could be her day off. "We agree that we won't tell anyone about Hugo, right?" I asked.

"I don't think we should say anything other than we have installed some cameras in front. We want this person to go to the back."

I nodded. "No mention of the person on the bike, right?"

Jaxson reached across the table and clasped my hand. "Stop worrying. It makes me more anxious and makes people think we have no idea what we're doing."

"Do we know what we're doing?"

Jaxson let go of my hand and leaned back. "Sometimes, Glinda, you have to trust others."

"I know."

Our server came over. We both knew what we wanted, so we ordered right away. "Do you think Rihanna will be able to get a reading off of a door handle?"

"Not if she doesn't know the person. Has she met Glen?"

I blew out a breath. "No, which might be a problem."

"Did you sign up for the two to four shift again for tonight?" Jaxson asked.

"I did, but it would be super if you came along again too."

"Then count me in."

"You are the best."

He winked.

Since I never spotted Dolly, we were able to eat our lunch without interruption, though knowing what she'd learned might have been useful. "After Rihanna does her thing, I want to pick Pearl's brain," I said.

He chuckled. "Why not talk to Steve directly?"

Really? "Pearl will actually tell me stuff."

"You might be right."

Once we finished and paid, we returned to the office. It wasn't long before Rihanna came home from school. "How was your day?" I asked.

"Good, but you don't have to ask every day. If it's bad, I'll tell you."

"Gotcha. If you aren't tired, we have something we'd like you to do for us."

Rihanna dropped her backpack onto the sofa. "What is it?"

I explained about seeing somebody testing each of the security doors last night. "But he didn't try to get in."

"Who was it?" she asked.

"That's what we're hoping you can tell us."

"Me?"

"Rihanna," Jaxson said. "You might get a reading off of one of the doors. They were installed yesterday, so not many people other than the installer, touched the knob. Can you give it a go?"

"Sure." She looked around. "Where's Iggy?"

"Where do you think?"

She sighed. "With Hugo. What's going to happen when we finish this case, and Hugo returns to his gargoyle form?"

"That is a problem, one that I'm hoping Iggy is prepared to handle."

"I hope Aimee is willing to support him emotionally."

I half smiled. "I hope so, too. Ready?"

"Yes."

The three of us went across the street to the Hex and Bones Apothecary. Instead of entering through the front, we walked via the alley to the back. We then let Rihanna do her thing.

"Which door did he touch?" she asked.

"All of them," Jaxson said. "Take your time. Glinda and I will wait back here."

Possibly to make sure I wouldn't try to take over, Jaxson wrapped a firm arm around my waist. For a change, I said nothing. I just watched Rihanna touch each handle. While there were signs next to each back door indicating which one belonged to which store, we didn't tell her the door that had been left open.

Rihanna spent a good thirty seconds at each site. When she finished, she returned. "I get the feeling I know this person."

That was exciting. "What did you see?"

"Nothing that will help. I just saw my English class."

"Is Wilt Harmony in that class?" Jaxson asked.

She stilled. "Yes, he is." Rihanna planted a hand over her mouth for a second. "You don't think he's involved do you? I mean, he said he set the fire to the bookstore, but no one believed him."

"I think he was covering for his brother," I said.

"Then why come here?"

"My guess would be to scope it out," Jaxson said.

She seemed to think about it for a moment. "Wow. Wilt must really care about his brother."

"Or else the father is driving them to seek revenge for him losing his livelihood," Jaxson said.

"I get it. Now what?"

I looked over at Jaxson. "Let's tell Steve what Rihanna learned."

"What about Iggy?" Rihanna asked.

"We'll see if he's ready to leave." I touched Jaxson's arm. "Did you think it was Wilt on the bike?"

"I did." He pulled up a note on his phone and showed me he'd written down his name.

"You are smart," I said.

"I hope that's not news to you."

I punched him in the arm. I didn't need him to get a big head.

We went around to the front and entered the shop. When I stepped into the back, Iggy rushed over to me. "What's wrong?" I asked.

"Hugo won't stay human forever."

I picked him up. "I know, but he'll come back—or reappear—when he can. He really likes you."

"I guess."

"Did you learn anything?"

"No. Hugo said he knows what to do, and I believe him."

"Okay. We need to chat with the sheriff, so I'm taking you with us."

"Fine." He turned around, told Hugo goodbye, and then wished him luck.

I'd love it if there was something Andorra could do to keep Hugo in his human form, but maybe it shortened his lifespan when he wasn't a gargoyle.

Jaxson, Rihanna, Iggy, and I descended on the sheriff's office. "Jaxson, why don't you and Rihanna tell Steve what you learned. I want to chat with Pearl."

"You got it."

As soon as they headed to the sheriff's office, I stepped over to the reception desk. "Hey, Pearl. Do we have coverage for tonight?"

She scanned her list. "Yup, assuming you are up for the two to four shift again."

"Jaxson and I will be there. Hear any scuttlebutt about the possibility of a fire at the store in order to take down Heath Richards?"

"No, and that is unusual. Someone is bound to hear something soon."

I really wanted to ask about Glen Harmony, but if he was innocent, I didn't want to give him more pain than he was already going through. "Keep up the great work. I hope if this arsonist plans on doing more harm, then he does it quickly."

"Amen."

Since Rihanna and Jaxson were with Steve, I headed back there. When I entered, Jaxson jumped up and motioned I take his seat. The sheriff needed to have some folding chairs that could be stacked against the wall for when he had more company. "What do you think?" I asked Steve.

"Since you didn't prompt Rihanna in any way, and she sensed her English class, it does seem as if Glen might be our man. I will spend the next few nights at the Hex and Bones, but I have to admit it's hard to fall asleep with a gargoyle staring down at me all night."

I couldn't help but laugh. "I am sorry. If it's any consolation, he creeps me out, too."

Iggy popped his head out of my purse. "Don't talk about Hugo that way."

I petted his head. "I'm sorry."

"Do you need me to do anything else, Glinda?" Steve asked.

"Nope."

"Let's all keep sharp again tonight."

We left, but I wasn't sure what else there was to do but wait. As much as I wanted to get started on the fundraiser, if word leaked out what we were doing, Glen—or whoever was the arsonist—might wait before striking again. If that happened, Steve would give up and sleep in his own bed.

"How about I skip school tomorrow and come watch the feed with you guys tonight?"

My first instinct was to say no way, but she was going to graduate in six weeks. She also was an adult and should be able to make her own decisions. "It will be boring."

"Not as boring as being in school. Do you know how hard this last month is going to be?"

I chuckled. "Yes. I didn't like high school much, but college was better."

"Great, but I'm not in college yet."

Iggy waddled over to us. "I want to come, too."

I suppose it wouldn't hurt. If he was tired, he'd crawl into a corner and fall asleep. "Fine. It will be one big party."

IT HONESTLY DIDN'T surprise me when Rihanna put her head down on the conference room table an hour into our surveillance and fell asleep. I looked over at Jaxson, but his gaze was focused on the back entrance. We had inside cameras turned on, but they showed very little, in part because it was rather dark in the store. It had to be that way or else it might tip off the arsonist. There were two Exit signs that glowed red, and Bertha had turned on one or two objects that cast light, allowing us to see someone's face—or at least we hoped.

It was three thirty, and I kept looking at my phone to see how much longer we had to wait when Jaxson nudged me.

"What?"

"Someone is approaching on foot. Naturally, his head is down, but from his size, I'd bet anything that it's Glen Harmony."

"Rihanna and Iggy. It's showtime," I said.

My cousin lifted her head. The moment she spotted him, she seemed to be on high alert. No one said anything. Good thing the cameras were recording this.

Glen—assuming that was who it was—pulled open the security door to the Hex and Bones—and picked the lock on the rear entrance door. He was inside in less than thirty seconds.

"I hope Hugo heard him," I said.

"He did," Iggy said. I hadn't even noticed he'd joined us.

While there was sound, our arsonist was quiet. Considering he wasn't carrying anything, it had to be our garage mechanic. I hoped it wasn't someone else—someone I liked and trusted.

He made a beeline to the front where Bertha had always kept the spell books. I bet that surprised him when he saw they were gone.

He pounded the table. "Mad much?" I asked.

"Maybe Glen is psyching himself up," Jaxson said.

"Are we sure it's Glen?" Rihanna asked.

"We'll find out in a moment if something bursts into flames."

The arsonist looked up for a moment, probably trying to figure out his next move.

"It's Glen!" I practically shouted it. I honestly don't know why I was so excited, other than if it had been someone we'd never seen before, then I'd feel like I'd failed somehow.

"Maybe I should cloak myself and go next door to help Hugo," Iggy said.

I totally understood that he wanted to get some of the glory, too, but if his cloaking failed, he could get hurt. "Please stay here."

It wasn't as if he could get out of this glass-enclosed room anyway.

Jaxson lifted up Iggy and held him close. My partner was a wonderful man.

Glen turned around. It looked as if he was going to leave, but partway to the door, he stopped and slipped a shirt off of a rack. It immediately burst into flames.

In two seconds, several more were on fire. "Where's Hugo?" My voice actually cracked.

I wasn't sure what happened next, exactly, but one second the flames were eating up the material, and the next they were extinguished.

Glen yelled and lifted his arms. While it was kind of hard to tell, it looked as if his hands were encased in something clear.

Steve came out of the back. "Glen Harmony, you are under arrest for arson."

No surprise, Glen took off running toward the back exit, but he stopped at the door. "Would you look at that. He can't open the door with his hands that way. I bet Steve knew that."

"Hugo would have stopped him anyway," Iggy said with a lot of cheer.

The back door opened, and Nash appeared. Had he been staying awake each night, too, or had Misty and her crew followed Glen to the stores and had given Nash a heads up?

The two officers escorted him outside. Since the lights in the back were bright, we could see Glen and his frozen hands. Steve looked back at the camera and smiled.

"We did it," I said.

Jaxson leaned over and kissed my cheek. "We did."

"Hugo was the hero, you know," Iggy said.

We all laughed. "He was at that."

Chapter Nineteen

"GLINDA, YOU DID an amazing job," Bertha said. We were in the park looking at all of the booths at the fair that would provide Heath Richards with enough money to fix up the stores and to keep them fixed up for quite some time. "I only organized things. The true star was my Aunt Fern and the other ladies. They did almost everything else."

"But you convinced the mayor to call in a few favors for the rides."

"Yes, but he wanted this to be a success as much as the rest of us."

Jaxson stepped next to me. "I spotted a fudge stand. Want to give it a try?"

He knew me so well. "Of course." I turned back to Bertha. "Your job is to make sure that Mr. Richards does what he promised to do."

"I'll make sure he does."

Two of Bertha's friends came over, so I didn't feel bad leaving her. "Fudge is my weakness, you know," I said to him.

He grinned. "You don't have to tell me."

We found the stand, and boy, did my mouth water. "Erin, this looks amazing."

She grinned. "Thanks. It's my Mom's recipe. I like to

make it every year to remember her by."

"That is so sweet. I'll take two pieces."

Erin placed them on paper and handed them to me while Jaxson paid. Since Maude had a stand, we went over to buy some drinks.

"There she is. Our coordinator queen," Maude said.

"Hardly. You ladies deserve all the credit."

"Thanks. I know it's a fundraiser, but we should do this every year. I'm sure we can find some use for the money raised."

"You are right. How's business?"

"Fabulous. I swear, I'm selling more today than I do in a week at the store."

"Good to hear."

She looked around. "I heard some gossip."

"About Glen?"

She waved a hand. "No, that's old hat. He's going to trial next week. I'm sure he'll be spending quite a long time in jail."

"I actually feel sorry for him."

Maude sighed. "I do, too, in a way. It's real tough when one of your parents is suffering. You want to seek justice for him, but Mr. Richards had no choice but to shut down that strip mall. Glen's daddy didn't have to drink so much. He could have handled the closing of the business better—for his children's sake.

"Is Mrs. Harmony around to be there for Wilt?"

"No. Poor dear passed away a few years ago. That family has had it tough. I heard it's why Glen went to that pseudo doctor to get help for his anger."

"A pseudo doctor?"

"I don't know what else to call him, but apparently, he

was supposed to do a spell to help Glen cope with life, but instead it gave him those powers. You saw what he could do."

"Yes. What a shame he didn't go to Bertha or someone reputable."

"I think he was embarrassed," she said.

That was such a shame. "What will happen to Wilt? He'll be graduating in a few weeks. What's he going to do?"

"I heard their dad found another job. I hope he sobers up for Wilt."

"Me, too."

"Any other gossip?" I asked.

"I heard that Mr. Richards has rented out the bookstore space already."

The place was still a mess. "I know the water has been cleaned up and everything cleared out, but it's in no shape to be used as a storefront."

She shrugged. "Apparently, this woman plans to gut the store—walls and everything—and start from scratch."

"That's smart," Jaxson said. "What kind of store is it?"

He was probably hoping for a computer store.

"A vintage candy store."

I grabbed Jaxson's hand and squeezed. "Really. That's fantastic. I love those places."

Jaxson laughed. "You love all things sweet."

"I know, but a candy store?" I turned back to Maude. "Who is the new owner."

"She's not from around here. Courtney somebody. That's all I know."

Heath Richards would have more information, and I bet he'd be willing to tell me everything. After all, Bertha and I saved him from financial ruin. "Thanks for the update."

Jaxson and I left to make the rounds. We stopped at Drake's booth. "I see you have a helper," I said to Drake. Andorra was with him.

"I do, and a fine helper she is."

No one was around, and since the whole issue with Hugo has been bothering me, I had to ask. "What do you think would happen if I brought Iggy by to see Hugo? Can your familiar communicate when he's in his gargoyle form? I mean, he must be aware of what's going on or else he wouldn't know when to transform into his human form, once he senses you're in danger."

Her brows pinched. "This will sound really, really strange, but I don't think I've tried to communicate with him when he's merely a statue. I know that's terrible of me, but when I left Witch's Cove, I knew I couldn't take him with me. He needs to remain in the store to stay alive—if that is even the right word."

"Why?"

"I can't say exactly. It was the first place I showed him. As soon as he stepped in here, he lit up. He told me all of the occult artifacts made him feel alive for the first time."

Maybe that was because he was alive for the first time. "You never took him home?"

"Oh, sure, but after a few hours, I could see the energy drain out of him, so I would take him back to the store. He would change into this statue form to recuperate. As time went on, he was in that form for longer and longer periods of time. Only if he thought I was in danger did he change again."

That didn't sound like a fun familiar. I would hate it if Iggy took another form for any length of time. "Good to know. How about the next time I stop in the store, I have Iggy with me? I know he's been a bit sad over his loss."

"I think that would be great."

"I, too, have a question," Jaxson said. "We have the video of Glen setting some of the shirts on fire. It's rather nice that we can't tell he isn't using a lighter to do it."

"I agree. I think any jury would convict him."

"How will the lawyers explain that the flames suddenly went out?" he asked.

She smiled. "Fire retardant material?"

I had the sense that wasn't true, but it made sense. "I trust they'll keep the video of Glen rushing to the door, but I wonder how they'll explain him suddenly stopping. Will he say his hands were encased in ice?"

"Excellent question," she said.

"Too bad you witches haven't learned how to selectively delete memories," Jaxson said.

That would be nice. "I'm sure Steve and the law team will figure something out. Besides, if Glen tries to worm out of it, we can use the tape of his brother scoping out the place."

Everyone nodded. "I bet Glen wouldn't want that to get out," Drake said.

"I bet he wouldn't either, but today should be a happy one. We need to celebrate our successes," I said.

Jaxson wrapped an arm around my waist. "I have just the thing. Come on."

He nodded to the Ferris wheel. I couldn't wait to share such a romantic overture with the man I adored and loved.

I hope you enjoyed Pink Smoke and Mirrors.

What's next? BROOMSTICKS AND PINK GUM-DROPS

Someone has rented the burned out bookstore and is renovating it. Never in a million years did this new owner expect to find a skeleton in the wall. Needless, to say Glinda is on the case, but when she and Jaxson find themselves back in Ohio in the 1970s again, her life is turned upside down.

Buy on Amazon or read for FREE on Kindle Unlimited

Don't forget to sign up for my Cozy Mystery newsletter *to learn about my discounts and upcoming releases. If you prefer to only receive notices regarding my releases, follow me on BookBub.*
http://smarturl.it/VellaDayNL
bookbub.com/authors/vella-day

Here is a sneak peek of **Broomsticks and Pink Gumdrops**

"GUESS WHO I met," my good friend announced with pride.

Penny Carsted and I used to waitress together at the Tiki Hut Grill. I loved it when Penny was excited. "The new owner of the yarn shop?"

"It sold? When? Have you met this person?"

I chuckled. "I hadn't heard if it has or hasn't sold. You said to guess, and I did."

"Oh, well guess again."

I had given her my one and only one suggestion. "I have no idea."

"Courtney Higgins."

I had to wrack my brains who that might be, but I failed to recall anyone by that name. For an amateur sleuth it was my job to know everyone in town. Apparently, I was off my game today. "Refresh my memory who that is."

Penny laughed. "You are a hoot, Glinda."

Uh-oh, that implied I should know her. After all, Witch's Cove only had a population of two thousand. *Think.* "I got it! The new owner of the soon-to-open candy store." It was where the burned out bookstore used to be.

"Good for you."

I waited for my little gossipy friend to fill me in, but she just smiled at me. "Fine. I'll beg. Spill."

Penny was on her ten-minute break, and even though she didn't have a lot of time, she pulled out the chair across from me and sat down. "Okay. Courtney is probably in her early thirties and is really cute. I didn't want to grill her too much, but I know she's from someplace in Ohio."

"Ohio, huh? Florida will be quite the change. Did she say why she decided to open a candy store?" I don't remember the last time I'd seen one—in any town.

"I didn't ask since I didn't want to come off as being overly curious."

Like me. "I get that. Did she say when she expects her store to open?" Paper had been plastered across the windows for several days now. Considering the amount of damage from the bookstore fire, she'd have to gut the place. Since she was renting, I imagine the building owner would help out with the rebuilding process since he received insurance money.

"No, but for your sake, I hope she opens soon." Penny knew what a sweet tooth I had.

"You and me both."

She pushed back her chair. "I'm afraid my break's over. The owner here is a tyrant."

I laughed. "For sure." That tyrant was my very lovable Aunt Fern.

"As one of the town's ambassadors, you should stop over and see if our new resident needs help with anything."

Penny just wanted to get the scoop. "So now I'm an ambassador?"

"I thought saying you were nosy didn't sound as good."

I couldn't help but grin. "You are right. I'll see what I can find out and let you know."

Penny giggled. "You're the best."

As I finished my meal, I decided I should visit Courtney to see if she needed anything. After all, with my connections to the town's main gossip queens, I could provide her with any information she needed. If she wanted help cleaning up, I could offer a hand, too. At the moment, my sleuth agency didn't have any customers, which meant I was free to do what I wanted.

In the past, every spare moment I had was spent waitressing in order to bring in more money to grow our company. Ever since the extremely bizarre event in which my partner, Jaxson, my cousin, Rihanna, and my familiar, Iggy, time traveled back to the 1970s for a few days over Christmas, we had more money than we needed. Long story short, we ended up being given a large thank you check.

Just as I was about to leave, my aunt came over to my table. "I see we have a new member in our community." She wiggled her eyebrows.

My Aunt Fern was one of the famous gossip ladies, mostly because one of her friends was the sheriff's grandmother, a woman who had her finger on the pulse of the town. "Did you speak with Courtney when she came in to eat?" I asked.

My aunt's eyes widened slightly. Aha. She hadn't expected I'd know that.

"I did. She is a lovely young lady."

"Besides the fact she is from Ohio, what did you learn?"

My aunt pulled out the same chair Penny had recently vacated. "She came to Witch's Cove because a fortune teller told her this was where she needed to be."

I might be a witch who believed in the talents of my fellow sorcerers, but to move half way across the country because some fortune teller told me to wasn't something I would have done. But what did I know about her circumstances? Nothing. "Does Courtney know anyone here?"

"Not a soul. She chose our Florida town because of its name."

I leaned forward. "Do you think that means she's a witch? I mean, why else come to Witch's Cove? She can't expect to make a killing at a candy store in a town our size." The name of her place was Broomsticks and Gumdrops, which implied she at least was open to witchcraft.

"During the high season, she'll do well."

"I hope so, but I know how much the bookstore struggled, regardless of the season."

"Candy is more popular than books these days," my aunt

said.

"I hope you're right."

My aunt stood. "We have to catch up."

"Totally."

She lived across the hall from me, but of late we seemed to be ships passing in the night since our hours didn't seem to coincide.

Even though my aunt told me that my food was on the house, I always paid. After promising to give her the lowdown, I headed across the street to meet our new resident.

It was possible only workers were inside the store and not the new owner, but if I didn't at least try to find out, I'd spend the night wondering what this Courtney Higgins person was like.

With a million questions ready, I knocked on the door's papered window. I could hear some banging inside, so when no one answered, I tried again, harder this time. And then I waited.

To my delight, a tall, beautiful brunette, pulled open the door, and suddenly, I forgot what I wanted to say.

Her eyebrows rose. "Yes?"

"Hello," was about all I could get out. And trust me. I was rarely at a loss for words. What caused me to be tongue-tied, I don't know. Maybe it was that Courtney was so young and pretty.

"Can I help you?"

"Courtney?"

"Yes."

The confirmation helped me regain my composure. "I was hoping I could help you."

She smiled. "Oh! Okay. Want to come in? Just know that the place is a total mess."

Come in were welcome words to a curious person. "Not a problem." I stepped inside and held out my hand. "I'm Glinda Goodall. My aunt owns the Tiki Hut Grill."

"I love the food there."

"Good to hear." I debated telling her I was an amateur sleuth, but I didn't want to overwhelm her right off the bat. I looked around her construction site. Two men were ripping down the walls—walls that had dingy, water-stained wallpaper on them. "This looks like it's going to take a lot of work."

"It will, but that's why the owner isn't charging me any rent until I open. I imagine it will be another few weeks before I'm ready to install the cabinets and shelving, and then I can order the candy and other paraphernalia."

"How nice of him to give you a price break. I hope he's paying for at least some if not all of the renovations."

"He is."

I tried to imagine this not being a bookstore, but I couldn't. I guess I'd have to wait until she opened to see what she had in mind. "I am curious why you chose to come to Witch's Cove."

Courtney glanced to the workers and then turned back at me. "It will sound stupid."

Aha. She wanted to talk about the fortune teller. Some were legit, others were not. "Once you get to know me, you'll realize I don't think anything is out of the realm of possibility."

"Really?"

"Really."

"Come into the back so we can chat. It's not as noisy in there."

The men were making quite a racket. In the other room, she had a small table set up with a computer on top. A microwave, as well as a dorm-sized refrigerator whose face was a bit blackened no doubt as a result of the smoke damage, sat on the counter.

"Want something to drink?" she asked.

"I'm good."

Courtney grabbed a soda out of her small fridge and sat down. "My story is strange sounding, even to me. First though, let me give you a brief history of the life of Courtney Higgins." She smiled.

"I'm all ears."

"I was engaged to this really great guy—or at least I thought he was a great guy. Long story short, he found another woman and told me he didn't think having an entrepreneur for a girlfriend was a good thing. When he dumped me, I'm not proud to say I kind of went on an emotional rollercoaster."

"Who wouldn't?" Jaxson was the first real boyfriend I'd had. If he decided he didn't want to be with me, I wasn't sure how I would cope.

"Right? Anyway, about three weeks after the breakup, I was with a few of my friends who convinced me to go to this local fair. It was a hokey little thing, but I knew there would be great fudge—something I can never say no to."

My heart zinged, and then I moaned. "I love homemade fudge."

When our town had a save-this-strip-of-buildings fundraiser, Jaxson bought me some of the rich, chocolatey confection, which I thought it was such a romantic gesture. That fair, especially its Ferris wheel ride, made for such a memorable day.

"Me, too. After we gorged on it, we saw this fortune teller. I wasn't going to have a session, but this woman told one of my friends a few things that were so dead on about her life that I had to give her a try."

"She told you to come to Witch's Cove?"

"Not exactly. She said that the only way to find true love was to leave behind the life I had and start anew."

I whistled. I believed in true love, so I couldn't tell her she was being foolish, but to move to a new town because someone suggested it? Even I wouldn't do that, and I've been tempted to do quite a lot of crazy things in my twenty-seven years. "I'm not sure I could pack up and leave my family."

"My parents were killed three years ago in a car accident, and I was an only child."

My heart cracked. "I am so sorry."

Her lips pressed together. "Thanks."

A change of topic was clearly needed. "Why Florida?"

"Have you ever been to Ohio in the winter?" she asked and then chuckled.

"I have. Once. I thought it was so beautiful when it snowed, but I understand that the cold might get old after a while. If this fortune teller suggested Florida, why Witch's Cove?" I was wondering if Courtney's story would match what she'd told Aunt Fern.

"The truth? I loved the name."

I really wanted to ask if she was a witch, but I thought

that was a bit too forward for having just met her. Not all witches were comfortable with their talents being known.

"If you ever want more hints about your future, we have the Psychics Corner right down the street. I can personally vouch for several of the people being authentic."

"You're saying they are actual witches?"

Her hint of surprise kind of implied she wasn't one. "Yup. Mind you I've never asked for a love spell or anything, but they have been able to contact the dead for me."

"For real?"

I might as well come clean. "My partner, Jaxson Harrison, and I run an amateur detective business. I bring it up because the person who knows the most about the murder is often the dead person." That wasn't always the case, but it was sometimes.

She stilled. "You're serious, aren't you?"

"As the day is long." Sheesh. Who said that anymore? I must be hanging out with the gossip queens too much.

I didn't feel comfortable enough to tell her that I'd seen ghosts and spoken with them. Nor would I mention I had a talking pink iguana who was my familiar since only witches had familiars.

"Maybe I'll see if I can talk to my parents then." Her bottom chin trembled. "Once I get settled, that is."

I couldn't imagine what life would be like without mine. "I bet it could help." I cleared my throat, needing a second to think of a something different to say. "So, do you have an artist's rendition of how you envision your store?"

Courtney seemed to shake herself out of her reminiscing, too. "I do."

She pushed back her chair, opened one of the soot-stained cabinets, and retrieved a rolled up piece of paper. "The real items I purchase may be different than this artist's sketch, but this will show you my vision."

When she unrolled it, I sucked in a breath. Looking at the vibrant colors and the massive amount of candy spiked my blood sugar. "Wow. That looks awesome."

"You think?" I nodded. She then tapped the paper. "In this corner, I want to have some Witch's Cove souvenirs, like T-shirts and stuff, for the tourists."

We have several stores that sold that kind of gear. "Since the name of your store is Broomsticks and Gumballs, why not sell witch stuff?"

"I guess I could. What do you think would sell?"

I didn't want her to compete too much with Hex and Bones Apothecary, but there were things that could be unique to her store. "Some small cauldrons, incense, and of course, small witchy broomsticks."

She grinned. "That's a great idea."

It was, wasn't it? Since the space was rather large, I wanted to offer another suggestion. "Have you thought of having a counter where you serve sodas and such? People might want to come here for date night. We have an ice cream shop in town, but that's about all."

"I'll definitely think about it."

The noise in the other room suddenly stopped. A moment later, someone knocked on the door, and a worker peeked his head in. "Ah, Miss Higgins?"

"Yes?"

"Sorry to bother you, but you gotta see this."

The worker's expression, along with his shaking hand, made me think he'd seen a ghost. We jumped up and dashed into the room where they'd finished tearing apart a partitioned wall. That in and of itself was not disturbing, but what took my breath away was what was inside the wall.

Courtney moved closer, and then faced the worker. "Is that what I think it is?"

"Yes, ma'am. Should we call the sheriff?"

Courtney looked over at me. "Glinda?"

"I'll run next door and let Steve know."

And here I thought I'd seen it all.

BUY ON AMAZON OR READ FOR FREE ON KINDLE
UNLIMITED

THE END

A WITCH'S COVE MYSTERY (Paranormal Cozy Mystery)
PINK Is The New Black (book 1)
A PINK Potion Gone Wrong (book 2)
The Mystery of the PINK Aura (book 3)
Box Set (books 1-3)
Sleuthing In The PINK (book 4)
Not in The PINK (book 5)
Gone in the PINK of an Eye (book 6)
Box Set (books 4-6)
The PINK Pumpkin Party (book 7)
Mistletoe with a PINK Bow (book 8)
The Magical PINK Pendant (book 9)
The Poisoned PINK Punch (book 10)
PINK Smoke and Mirrors (book 11)
Broomsticks and PINK Gumdrops (book 12)
Knotted Up In PINK Yarn (book 13)
Ghosts and PINK Candles (book 14)

SILVER LAKE SERIES (3 OF THEM)
(1). HIDDEN REALMS OF SILVER LAKE

(Paranormal Romance)
Awakened By Flames (book 1)
Seduced By Flames (book 2)
Kissed By Flames (book 3)
Destiny In Flames (book 4)
Box Set (books 1-4)
Passionate Flames (book 5)
Ignited By Flames (book 6)
Touched By Flames (book 7)
Box Set (books 5-7)

Bound By Flames (book 8)

Fueled By Flames (book 9)

Scorched By Flames (book 10)

(2). FOUR SISTERS OF FATE: HIDDEN REALMS OF SILVER LAKE (Paranormal Romance)

Poppy (book 1)

Primrose (book 2)

Acacia (book 3)

Magnolia (book 4)

Box Set (books 1-4)

Jace (book 5)

Tanner (book 6)

(3). WERES AND WITCHES OF SILVER LAKE

(Paranormal Romance)

A Magical Shift (book 1)

Catching Her Bear (book 2)

Surge of Magic (book 3)

The Bear's Forbidden Wolf (book 4)

Her Reluctant Bear (book 5)

Freeing His Tiger (book 6)

Protecting His Wolf (book 7)

Waking His Bear (book 8)

Melting Her Wolf's Heart (book 9)

Her Wolf's Guarded Heart (book 10)

His Rogue Bear (book 11)

Box Set (books 1-4)

Box Set (books 5-8)

Reawakening Their Bears (book 12)

OTHER PARANORMAL SERIES
PACK WARS (Paranormal Romance)
Training Their Mate (book 1)

Claiming Their Mate (book 2)

Rescuing Their Virgin Mate (book 3)

Box Set (books 1-3)

Loving Their Vixen Mate (book 4)

Fighting For Their Mate (book 5)

Enticing Their Mate (book 6)

Box Set (books 1-4)

Complete Box Set (books 1-6)

HIDDEN HILLS SHIFTERS (Paranormal Romance)
An Unexpected Diversion (book 1)

Bare Instincts (book 2)

Shifting Destinies (book 3)

Embracing Fate (book 4)

Promises Unbroken (book 5)

Bare 'N Dirty (book 6)

Hidden Hills Shifters Complete Box Set (books 1-6)

CONTEMPORARY SERIES
MONTANA PROMISES
(Full length contemporary Romance)

Promises of Mercy (book 1)

Foundations For Three (book 2)

Montana Fire (book 3)

Montana Promises Box Set (books 1-3)

Hart To Hart (Book 4)

Burning Seduction (Book 5)

Montana Promises Complete Box Set (books 1-5)

ROCK HARD, MONTANA

(contemporary romance novellas)

Montana Desire (book 1)

Awakening Passions (book 2)

PLEDGED TO PROTECT

(contemporary romantic suspense)

From Panic To Passion (book 1)

From Danger To Desire (book 2)

From Terror To Temptation (book 3)

Pledged To Protect Box Set (books 1-3)

BURIED SERIES (contemporary romantic suspense)

Buried Alive (book 1)

Buried Secrets (book 2)

Buried Deep (book 3)

The Buried Series Complete Box Set (books 1-3)

A NASH MYSTERY (Contemporary Romance)

Sidearms and Silk(book 1)

Black Ops and Lingerie(book 2)

A Nash Mystery Box Set (books 1-2)

STARTER SETS (Romance)

Contemporary

Paranormal

Author Bio

Love it HOT and STEAMY? Sign up for my newsletter and receive MONTANA DESIRE for FREE. smarturl.it/o4cz93?IQid=MLite

OR Are you a fan of quirky PARANORMAL COZY MYSTERIES? Sign up for this newsletter. smarturl.it/CozyNL

Not only do I love to read, write, and dream, I'm an extrovert. I enjoy being around people and am always trying to understand what makes them tick. Not only must my romance books have a happily ever after, I need characters I can relate to. My men are wonderful, dynamic, smart, strong, and the best lovers in the world (of course).

My Paranormal Cozy Mysteries are where I let my imagination run wild with witches and a talking pink iguana who believes he's a real sleuth.

I believe I am the luckiest woman. I do what I love and I have a wonderful, supportive husband, who happens to be hot!

Fun facts about me

(1) I'm a math nerd who loves spreadsheets. Give me numbers and I'll find a pattern.

(2) I live on a Costa Rica beach!

(3) I also like to exercise. Yes, I know I'm odd.

I love hearing from readers either on FB or via email (hint, hint).

Social Media Sites

Website:
www.velladay.com

FB:
facebook.com/vella.day.90

Twitter:
@velladay4

Gmail:
velladayauthor@gmail.com

Printed in Great Britain
by Amazon

59974802R00121